Chipmunka Anthology Volume Six

Chipmunka Anthology Volume Six

Chipmunka Anthology Volume Six

Introduction

Welcome to the Sixth Chipmunkapublishing anthology. We have decided to publish Chipmunkapublishing's shorter books in paperback so that we can give a voice to more people. It is our commitment to our authors that every Chipmunkapublishing title can end up having their work featured in paperback. Some of these books are quite short and would not be long enough to feature on their own as a paperback so putting several stories together enables books that may have only been e-books to come out as paperbacks. This anthology has 10 books inside it.

One Woman's Story
There was something about my dad
Graffiti Noir
Through the Eyes of a Manic
Colonies
My Fight Against A Life Of Depression
Clarissa: or arrested development.
The Lost Highway
Mashed Mind
A Victim of the Freemasons

Chipmunka Anthology Volume Six

SCHIZOPHRENIA: ONE WOMEN'S STORY

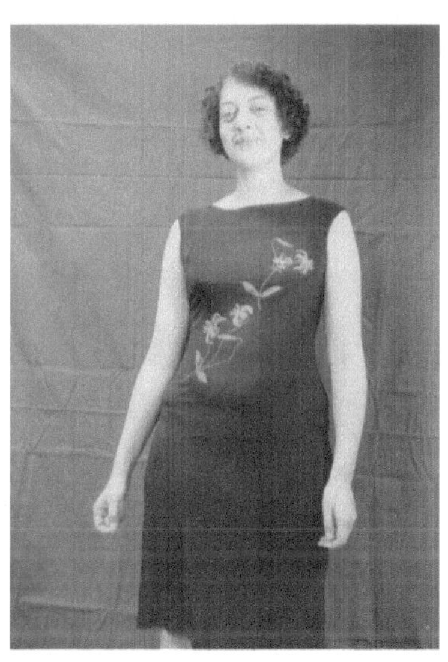

BY TIFFANY SUTTON

'One million people commit suicide every year.'
The World Health Organization

Chipmunka Anthology Volume Six

Published by
Chipmunkapublishing
PO Box 6872
Brentwood
Essex CM13 1ZT
United Kingdom

http://www.chipmunkapublishing.com

Proof-read by Anna Gomez

SCHIZOPHRENIA: ONE WOMAN'S STORY

LONDON E8

LONDON E5

RIVERSMEET: HERTFORD TOWN

BURGHFIELD COMMON

CHOLSEY

REVOLVING DOOR

BELGIUM

MARYLEBONE

READING

LONDON E8

Aged six months I was registered at Sunbabies nurseries. I played with a little Indian lad called David. Mum went to her work as a legal secretary, which in those days was an emancipated line of work. We lived on the 'J'1' floor, somewhere between Shoreditch and Dalston, I made friends with two girls: Christine Judge and Debbie. We would collect ring pulls from cans for charity. I used the telephone for the first time from Christine's place to 'phone Mum, it was scary. One night I stayed at Debbie's; I ate too much and asked if I could touch her Mum's hair – it looked so fantastic. I was surprised to find it was all stiff – my Mum's hair is so soft.

My Mum had these fabulous yellow and black shiny patent leather shoes. I would totter around in these fascinated by their shininess.

Our flat was beautiful: we had a bright orange sofa and black & white patterned wallpaper. One night, Mum brought Dad home: they got married; he took me on age four. He said, "Do you want Bricks or a doll?" I thought for a moment, and said "Bricks". So they got me a little toy pram and I would carry my bricks in it on various trips to the park.

Aged about six years I had seen "Oliver Twist", "Star Wars", "Jungle Book" and "Fantasia", at the cinema. I wanted to run away from home and thought about living on my wits like Oliver, but I decided that was not the safest idea, and I was too young.

I would put the encyclopaedia on the floor, and instead of reading the words, I would jump from one to another like stepping stones.

I had started school when I was four. The school was in Islington, I didn't like it much. Mum and I would go by bus, it was near her work. The cost of the bus-ride was only three pence.

I was bullied by a horrible little girl, but I had a nice friend called Lisa. I would go to her house after school and we would hide from the Daleks behind the sofa. The funny thing was, she wasn't scared. When Mum would come to take me home, I would hide under Lisa's sister's cot.

I remember thinking*: how will I ever make it to adulthood, what with being bullied, finding my Mum's husband difficult to get on with, and so on.* But I knew I could make it if only I could be strong.

At that young age I thought to myself about jumping out of the 7^{tlt} floor window, to avoid a possibly difficult future, but I couldn't bring myself to do it.

LONDON E5

We went to Greece. Mum made me a rainbow-striped top and trousers; I had a blue swimsuit and ran into the sea every morning. The hotel was on the beach, we ate octopus and drank ouzo. I ventured into the hotel disco: three men were dancing wildly, so I ran out scared. Mum and Dad thought this was amusing. We visited the Parthenon and the Acropolis in Athens, I wore a red poncho. We walked into the countryside; it was a hot day, three old gentlemen were playing with worry beads. I thought they were angels. Another day we walked for miles to a place called Marathon. The weather was terribly cold that day; we walked into the deserted hills and eventually came to a cafe where we ate. I wondered if we had left civilization. A few days later I went out with Mum and Dad under the stars, Dad tried to point the Milky Way out to me, but I couldn't see it just by looking up at it! Mum and Dad had walked on ahead of me.

Our little family had now moved from our flat in Cedar Court to Elderfield Road. We visited the pie and mash shop in Dalston, loved the steak pie and the green liquor, mashed potatoes, but could not eat eels. I thought they were alive: swimming in the tray.

At school I practised swimming and my parents were very proud – I managed eight hundred metres.

Then came the first signs of things not being quite right: one night on my way home from school I saw a strange old lady who passed me while r was waiting for my bus home; she had the strangest cold eyes and I was scared. It was dark. Just before we moved again my friend Christine East had the same look, I felt I was pushing out on a boat to dark unknown territory.

When we were in London, my family and I would visit Selfridges every year. We would also go to the Lord Mayor's Show; enchanted with the display we waved our flags in the icy cold. Nanny took me to shows in the West End, one year we went to see "The King and I" at the London Palladium.

When Mum gave birth to my brother and I was allowed to see him, I thought him so sweet and quiet with a lovely little smile on his face... I was astonished at his blue and green poo. I was told that was normal for a newborn, and thought of

John Lennon's song "Beautiful Boy".

I gathered bits and pieces about my identity: who I was; where I came from, along the way. Mum told me that my great-grandparents on Nanny's side had been killed in the concentration camps. My great-grandfather, Moritz, had been in a wheelchair and Golda; my great grandmother had stayed with him – they had been killed in the camps. Their four children had escaped via kinder transport. Nanny and Aunty Ruth had come to England, John went to Australia, and all they heard of Renata was that she would have no contact with Nanny and Ruth because they had married out of the Jewish faith. I felt that this was unfair, but in later years I understood how tradition was and still is very important. This is to make sure young Jewish people don't suffer for "wandering off" away from the faith.

Golda and Moritz, as I gathered from photographs, were extremely smart and clever and, until rounded up for the camps they had run a successful hardware store. However, I only picked this information up bit by bit over the years.

Mum and Dad were just starting out in Elderfield Road: that was their first house together; they had to pay the mortgage and were short on cash. Mum made homemade hummus with chick-peas and garlic. Nan used to bring round bags full of gifts for us, hand-knitted jumpers and sweets.

I looked forward to autumn because of my birthday and also because of November the fifth – an excuse for celebrations and bonfires. Every November fifth we would have a fire in the back garden, drink wine and put big potatoes in foil and cook them in the ashes. Mum discovered a recipe for 'parkin', a flapjack type sweet. My birthday was on the fifteenth and my brother's was on the ninth. After that, of course, came Christmas. Every Christmas there was a pillowcase of presents, intermingled with Satsuma and nuts and things.

Nanny would cook the most fabulous 'riboplatzien', which was basically a potato cake with onion, flour and other secret ingredients. To this day I have never tasted anything better.

I am very grateful to my Dad Kevin for helping me to make friends at Elderfield. I was typically shy, and one day, a short time after his sister, Aunty Andrea, had given me her bicycle, he winked at me and told me to "go out – there's some girls playing up the road", so with his insistence, I left the house and cycled the short distance uphill, and made friends with the two girls who were there. Coincidentally, they were called Christine and Debbie.

There followed one of the happiest periods of my life, I had friends! We all cycled off round the block, I was about nine years old. The friendship lasted until we had to leave London and I was fourteen.

We would do all sorts of things, visit Roman road for clothes, make a tent with material we found in a skip, hold it up in the middle with a broom-handle and play cards and eat sandwiches and drink milk brought out by Debbie's Mum. We would cycle round the block and in the holidays play in the schoolyard, where the boys would squirt us with water from washing-up plastic tubes. We would also go swimming and once Debbie got a cramp and I had to pull her to the side of the pool – she said I'd saved her life.

There was a lad called Andy who played with us at the pool, when he asked me out, my shyness took over and I realised that I really wasn't prepared for puberty. It was just dreadful; like one of those things I had wondered when I was five, whether I would ever make it through to adulthood.

Debbie, Christine and I went to the "Bethnal Green Museum of Childhood." Trying to find information we visited the Citizen's Advice Bureau, only to be told by an old man sitting there: 'you need tourist information'. It was so funny, but we were just scared.

We would go to the West End by bus; it was about ten pence for 'under sixteen'. We would see an old man that was always there, walking with his sandwich board, carrying the inscription. 'The End Is Nigh', he would say, and this provoked in us religious ponderances – which was slightly worrying.

Chris, Debbie and I would go to Church most Sundays: a Youth Club and a Sunday School were held there.

To be honest, that was a bit strange too. I am Jewish and it wasn't for me – I found Church frightening and didn't understand it.

Many years later I watched a television programme about Churches. The TV presenter showed a building: over the arch of the door was the inscription "This place is terrible". With the benefit of hindsight I would have run from the place like jolly nine pence. Instead, I think I was fascinated, caught in the grip of something larger than myself. So until we moved to the country I went to Church.

Something I discovered in my reading of the Old Testament was that a person isn't considered to be Jewish for ten generations if their parents aren't married, even though they actually are. Maybe that is why I felt pressured in Church.

It was really a question of whether I would stay sane or not. My personal spiritual identity was in question, not something I had found, something I had discovered, something new, but rather something my family had believed for aeons, something I had no choice about, but which was part of me (if one parent is Jewish, you are Jewish too).

For me, living a good life stemmed from being an upright citizen (Jewish people stand for something, from dusk until dawn, stand, all through the night). A person can't walk very well on their knees, let alone dance. Mum's friend Judy put it very well when she said to me: "each man must dance to the music he hears". Everything sterns from this: physicality or self-respect, cleanliness, the art of self-decoration, all stemmed from knowing who I was – my personal identity. Even expressing desire, feeling, all this I should have known in order to be myself, and to be safe.

RIVERSMEET

When I was fourteen years old, my family moved to an almost new terraced house in Hertfordshire, about twenty miles north of where we were before in London. I didn't like the area and felt like a plant that had been uprooted. I went to the local secondary school, but found it hard to make friends. I ended up sobbing on my bed for weeks at the life I had left behind. I felt terrible pain and didn't really get on with the other school kids. I perceived them as middle-class. Hertfordshire was strange to me. I felt culture shock – green fields everywhere; it was only a small town. We'd had to relocate because of Dad's job and I had wanted to stay with Nanny in Clapton – Hackney, but Mum had brooked no opposition and had told me: "you're coming with us". There are three life events said to be most likely to lead to a mental breakdown:

1)Housemove 2) Divorce

3) Bereavement

4) (Perhaps I can add, from a personal point of view):

Religious mania and too much drinking and partying!

Well, I had suffered a house move at a difficult age. Next thing I knew, my Granddad visited us at Riversmeet and I found out he was suffering with cancer of the pancreas. I was sad and scared, the family sat round the table. Granddad's face was shiny and clean, and suddenly I started to cry and felt like I was breaking up inside. I think that was the last time I saw him, Aunty Helen nursed him until his death a short while later.

I remember my Granddad for many things: his huge cigars; his dancing; his charisma; his beautiful shiny brown skin; the love I had for him in spite of all he may have done; the way he looked at me in the rear-view mirror of his car for minutes with happy bright eyes, until I jumped and realised I was being observed. I remember our visits to Bolton, where he lived and worked, and where he was accustomed to going to the "Black Man's Club" to play dominoes. I remember the war-time picture of Granddad in his long coat in the winter snow, on the back he had written: 'eternally yours'. He flew for the RAF, having seen and responded to a poster in Guyana with the caption "Your Mother Country Needs You!"

A defining memory of mine during this period was watching "The Way We Were" with my Mum one dark evening. The film starred Robert Redford and Barbra Streisand. I felt so distanced from Mum, as if she thought I was all grown-up and didn't need her anymore. The truth was I needed her more than ever, having been uprooted and finding it difficult to make mends, I felt she was being cool towards me and lacking in understanding. The fact is I was quite lost and Church hadn't helped.
Things got better at school and I became friends with a girl called Carolyn. She is a very sweet person who invited me into her home and did very well in life, going to Exeter to study French. We kept in touch for a while, and then as my illness came on I lost touch with her. I had two other girlfriends: Miranda, known as Muff, and Marcelle. They were great fun and we would drink cider, smoke, play cards, stay up all night... I suppose, looking back, all that partying may have made some impact upon my mental health. I was studying hard and had a Saturday job too.

BURGHFIELD COMMON

By the time I was sixteen, we had to move again – Dad had been offered a job near Reading. We were to have a house on a crossroads in a quiet village called Burghfield Common.

At that time I was questioning the meaning of life, reading Holy Scriptures, and trying to find my place in life and society. Having done very well for my age – sixteen exams, I decided to take A-Levels. Daniel was seven and a very sweet, kind, and loving boy, too. He was at the stage of knocking things off shelves; I would get annoyed and not let him into my room.

What followed was to be the most terrible period of my life. I actually became severely ill. I had no inkling of what was about to hit me. All I was really concentrating on was my A-Levels. Although the school was nearby in the village, it was in pleasant surroundings and I felt it was nice to be in the countryside, I was full of hope for the future. I had started going to Church, again.

One day I looked at a boy. He was painting the walls of the sixth form common room (most of us were). It was summer. I thought he was really good looking. He looked back at me and suddenly I was scared and moved away from my seat. I think he thought it was some kind of sexual come-on, although I was just admiring the scenery. I thought no more about it.

Then, while I was wandering around and in my own world, he started to really try it on with me. He would sidle up to me and stand really close, breathing down my neck and rubbing up against me. Well, you could say, I literally went mad. This lasted about two weeks and by then my clothes were dirty, my self-esteem had really gone down, and I hadn't really lived, I had not given a reaction. The lad had not said a word. What he needed was a slap on the face or a quick knee in the groin; it literally amounted to sexual harassment. A terrible pain exploded in my chest. Nanny thought it was a broken heart. I thought all I needed was a cuddle from Mum and I'd be alright.

Weird, eerie voices started coming from the radio, even when it was switched off. I had an identity crisis, the voices were telling me I was someone else and that I was doomed. 'Mum, help me', I said, and I was taken to the GP. He diagnosed me as suffering from schizophrenia I was sent to an adolescent unit, where I was given medication which I thought was inappropriate as it didn't seem to do anything to help me. All I remember of this time are some kind nurses and some lovely visitors. There are parts of my life that I can't remember.

CHOLSEY

It was hell on earth. I would describe suffering from schizophrenia as a cross between having cancer and living in a haunted house – it is terrifying. I wanted to sleep in Mum and Dad's bed but that wasn't appropriate, the GP had sent me to an adolescent unit. It wasn't the university experience I had hoped for. Instead of spreading my wings I had become someone who needed looking after like a child again.

A nice young man visited me and suggested I had been a victim of black magic. I said I didn't know anyone who did that sort of thing.

At the age of eighteen I was moved to an adult mental hospital. The nurses seemed like jailers. I was forcibly given medication. Somehow I couldn't believe I had an illness, yes, I was in great distress.

There was a period of observation: schizophrenia is an umbrella term for about eleven different types of illness; there are those people who have one episode and get better, not having to take medication again. There are those who need medication for life in order to stay out of hospital. Due to the side-effects and consequent 'lack of compliance' they can become 'revolving-door patients'. Yet others have face years in hospital because tablets and injections don't seem to work. There are very few whose illness makes them violent.

I was made to feel lucky because, apparently, the medications worked for me. However, I thought I was just being myself and couldn't differentiate

between my bouts of illness or periods of 'health'. What I really understood was that I was being periodically locked up for months on end, and this I perceived as a miscarriage of justice.
I have been hospitalised approximately fifteen times across the past twenty years. Thankfully, I was able to attend tribunals after three months of six-month sections.
Present at the tribunal are a Doctor, a Lawyer and a Layperson. These people were very kind and intelligent; they would usually let me go after three months, recognising that at times we felt like butterflies pinned down. For example, when receiving injections in the backside, an unruly patient would be held down by several members of staff.
Getting these injections was a horrible experience that felt a bit like being attacked or raped. On one occasion I was out for the count for about four days.

On the wards it was running battles: patients would look after and comfort each other, the nurses and patients just didn't see the best sides of one another. I think they thought of us as different species. At the end of the day, of course, staff could go home, but patients were there twenty-four hours. Besides, nurses chose to be in that line of work.
In recent years, however, the barriers have broken down a lot and patients and nurses are generally agreed that it's the bloody doctors who are the

problem. This, of course, is easier, as there are fewer of them and they are paid so ruddy much to make the decision about whether or not to lock someone up. It is not a nurse's decision to keep someone on a section, and nowadays patients and nurses are engaging and communicating with each other much more easily and to greater effect than before.

REVOLVING DOOR

So, for the past twenty years I have been a 'revolving door' patient. There are parts of my life I don't remember too clearly as in Barbra Streisands's famous song, "What is too painful to remember we simply choose to forget". However, I have had some times of great happiness, fun and success. I have lovely parents, brother and extended family. I have also met some very special people both in and away from hospital. I have managed to hold several jobs: I was a care worker for two years; I have been an artist's model; I have worked as a clerk, and I have also worked in a bar. Moreover, I have studied with the Open University. I've been a painter and decorator, a gardener and a cleaner. Once, when I was short of cash, I painted pictures for people on the ward (staff and patients) and raised about £100.

Of all the occupations, I think I enjoyed the bar work: I met a nice man called Michael there and the boss was a big, round man with curly hair.

Later, on one of the occasions that I was hospitalised I met a man called Michael. I was quite struck by him: he was tall, fair, had beautiful powder blue eyes, and was wearing an orange T-shirt and blue jeans. He fixed it up with the staff so that we could go home together. There began a short-lived passionate romance. I was so happy… I felt I had finally grown-up. However, after about three months I slung him out, as I was so angry at his violent behaviour towards me.

Somehow, in my befuddled thinking, I thought he was the Michael from the bar: when I went to the shop and brought back about ten bottles, he said: 'that's more like it'.

We hardly ever spoke. But, actually, we had a lot in common. He told me he'd been a dustman and had done an O.U course, the same course I had done. I loved him so much. But perhaps it wasn't meant to be.

When I was re-admitted to hospital after throwing my tablets down the loo, he visited me. And he wrote me a lovely poem and gave me a small wooden cross.

My illness just seemed to be getting worse. I attributed my anger and emotions of rage to the pre-menstrual syndrome. I suffered from PMS for years, sometimes I wonder if people just thought of me as a dreadful woman, unable to control my terrible emotions.

Mentally, I was considered deluded. I wondered whether I had been different characters in past lives. I thought I had been an African princess who had become Henry VIII's mistress. At other times I thought I had been the Impressionist painter: Monet.

There was a time in hospital (after Michael) when I attempted to turn over a big toaster and set my sheets on fire in the hope that the hospital would burn down. I didn't consider people's safety and vaguely assumed that everyone would get out. It was a gesture towards the condemnation of the dreadful place it was.

The attempt to burn the place down did not succeed, I was frogmarched over to the secure unit. It was night. There was no music. It was called a low-stimulus ward. I went about eight months locked behind double steel doors without a tune.

Schizophrenia is the strangest disease: it can make a person feel so alone. One time I was on a bus. I was sitting upstairs at the front, looking out at the scenery and my handbag started to talk to me, or to put it another way, I was hearing voices coming from my handbag. I turned around and asked the people behind me if they had heard anything and the people who were there just ignored me and stared straight. I felt terribly alone and frightened. By then the pain was gone.

Another time I was sitting outside St. Mary's Church, opposite the market-place in Reading and a tall lamppost was there, with the bus's time-table on it. I was sitting near it on a wall outside the Church and I started hearing voices from it. How strange. It seemed very real.

I lived in a care home for a while and worked from there.

By 1994 the local council had given me a flat. I decorated it but was very young and found it hard looking after myself. Although I had some great friends I was a bit vulnerable. Andy, Michaela and Mo, among others, would take me out to eat, to art galleries, dancing, music events... We would take the train to London, to Bournemouth or we would just stay in. Those were difficult times for me, even if it looked good on the surface.

BELGIUM

One night I was alone in my flat, and I knew I had to get away; I had decided I didn't want to stay in Newbury. I didn't want to die there, so even though I had a lifelong tenancy on the flat, I wasn't happy with it and I just walked out. Michael's essence was everywhere.

It was midnight and I was walking along a road heading to Chieveley Service Station. It was wet, the cars' headlights passed and I knew I would have to walk only a few miles. When I got there the cafeteria was fairly deserted, so I went outside and asked a few truck drivers if I could cadge a lift. I said I was going towards Dover. Eventually, a Turkish man said to get on board. I was so tired but kept awake. When we got to Dover I hid in the back of the huge truck petrified in case I got caught: I didn't have a passport. We got through customs because they didn't know I was there, and I could sit up again in the passenger seat. The driver was a fantastic person and, as soon as we got through customs he bought me the most delicious chicken-dinner. I was really hungry and thought him very kind.

Day came, and we were in France. There were trucks around again, and I got a lift with a man in a smaller truck. He said he could take me to Antwerp. On the way we passed Flanders Fields and he talked about the Congo and what was happening there. Flanders seemed like huge green acres of land. I didn't even see any poppies; there was no trace of what had happened there.

Finally we arrived in Antwerp. I was so tired I

decided to stop there, although I didn't have too good a feeling about the place.
I found a deserted building with no roof and puddles on the floor. I sat down and took a breather. It was cold. I picked up my Bible and big, furry coat and walked towards the town centre. I was so tired... People in the main square directed me to a Youth Hostel. When I got there it was dark. A nice young man called Stan agreed to give me a job cleaning for a few hours a day in exchange for a bed. They fed me cheese sandwiches and for a few days I did the cleaning. Then they gave me a job looking up streets on maps. I was very happy. It just felt nice to be in a better place. The people were nice; there was a kind of international vibe.

After a week or two I had to leave. I decided, responsibly, that I had to get back to England for my fortnightly injection. It was so depressing, I thought, if it weren't for this illness I could have worked my way around the world, I could have done so much.
One of the guys at the hostel told me about his experiences as a gangster, I was so frightened it added to my need to get away.
I left in the morning. The police picked me up walking along the motorway. I didn't tell them anything. They put me on a ferry back to England. I nearly jumped overboard because I was convinced I was being abducted to be a Mafia wife. Of course I wasn't. My Bible stopped me from jumping to a watery grave. I hitched back.

I then spent approximately three years in a hospital that was to close down. That was one of the happiest times of my life. I felt so clued up and clever, I thought we were political prisoners. Then I decided I couldn't take any more hospitalisation and decided to comply with medication.

I spent some months in a care home – Yew Tree Lodge. It was awful, and I ended up back in hospital.

Now the strangest thing comes. I was in a ward in the new hospital. The atmosphere was horrible, and I felt, as a particularly vindictive nurse had told me years before, that I was hated by both staff and patients. Although I hope she has been proved wrong.

I was shot in the head, in the toilet, on Daisy Ward. As I was sinking to the floor I looked up, and. seeing 'Tif' I scrawled towards the door and that is all I remembered of that moment.

Next thing I know I'm in the communal area being held down by two nurses. Something happened in my behind. It was probably an injection, although I suspected they were putting a bug in my behind, or even raping me.

When I regained consciousness again 1 was in the police station being held down by about six policemen, trying to get off the blue mat. Lucy, my social worker, came and talked to me through the window of the cell and eventually I was released.

They put me in a white van, and I'm being taken to the hill at the top of the town. I'm told that I will be living there for a while. The place is horrible, I'm scared, I run out, down the hill, run and run and run until I reached the town centre of Reading. There are lights there. I think about jumping in the luggage compartment of a roach but everything is moving too quickly. I get back, eventually, to the hospital and I'm put on Sorrell ward, I can't stay on Daisy Ward. Safe, secure, I sleep.

I prayed for three solid days to be released to go back home to Reading. By October I was told I was going back home.

MARYLEBONE

Soon after my admission to Sorrell Ward, the secure unit in the new Reading hospital, I was dispatched off to a hospital in Marylebone London. I was frightened: my Mum and Dad were not told of my move until I had gone, and I didn't know if or when I was returning. I was escorted in a car to London, convinced that the lady who was accompanying me was St. Mary Magdalene. In my mind I had divided the staff on Sorrell Ward into 'Saints and Sinners': there was Idi, Amin, Hesse, St Thomas, and so on. It was the humour needed to survive and make sense of the situation.

When we arrived at the hospital in London I met the member of staff who was in charge there: I was sure he was Allah.

Many of the staff wore squared-toe shoes; I thought this meant they were witches, as in the Roald Dahl books. It was awful being so far from home. Mum and Dad visited every week, which helped because some of the patients were a bit bossy. I learned to retreat to my room and made friends with a nice woman called Danny. She said she was a shepherd, was very sweet and gave me a jacket and some flip-flops, which were in fashion at the time.

I spent four months in Marylebone, and went outside twice: once to Regent's Park and once to try, unsuccessfully, to cash a giro.

It was quite frightening there, and although the food was very nice I got it into my head that the staff were killing us at night and serving us up for dinner the next day. Yet, somehow we were resurrected

the following day
My ideas were rather confused: I was convinced that Jesus was living in the hospital with his disciples. We were allowed to go downstairs to the inner garden on occasions. There was a tall, thin man wearing sandals, jeans and an over-sized jumper. He was very thin – I thought he was Jesus. I would sometimes look out over the garden and watch a man rolling cigarettes – thought he was St Thomas and that he had come to see me.
It was very strange being at Marylebone hospital at times: for example, there was a woman on my floor who was the spitting-image of my Mum. She was mixed-race, with an afro hairstyle, same height, everything. The main difference was that my Mum was a lot cleaner. I decided that the strange woman was Muff – my friend from school – who had been caught in an imaginary fire that had made her skin brown.
There was also a young woman who I thought looked like my eldest cousin, whom I hadn't seen in years.
Then, one night in the smoking room one of the women showed me a photo she had taken of me. It was exactly like me, except that for in the picture my eyes looked blue. My eyes are brown.
All this was very unsettling.

READING

We drove back to Reading. I was enormously relieved to be in one piece.

This time I was admitted to Rose Ward. My diagnosis was modified to "schizoeffective disorder" and I was put on clozapine.

I was still suffering from hallucinations. At night I saw visions of snakes, it was so horrible. It was so frightening; I had to attribute what I was going through to my illness. I would run around the ward at night screaming for the lights to be switched on. Once or twice a nurse locked me in my room, and then locked the outer door to the communal area as well, I thought of St Paul and the doors opened by themselves, (I had met him earlier, not recognizing him I had spat at him, thank goodness he had been wearing a scarf), I felt honoured to have met him.

It's a kind of twilight zone, being diagnosed as mentally ill. It's kind of good to be free to believe what we like. However, this experience of being classified as mentally unwell has been going on for me for so long now, I hope to stay out of hospital, and stay well.

THERE WAS SOMETHING ABOUT MY DAD

By

Maggie McDonagh (nee O'Brien)

'One million people commit suicide every year'
The World Health Organization

Chipmunka Anthology Volume Six

Published by
Chipmunkapublishing
PO Box 6872
Brentwood
Essex CM13 1ZT
United Kingdom

http://www.chipmunkapublishing.com

Edited by Jurita Bennett

Order of cover photo:

Left-right sitting: my dad Paddy and me (aged 8) on his lap, my mum Sarah and my late sister Bridie

Left-right back row standing: my brother Tom and my sister Eileen and next to me and my Dad my brother Martin.

In loving memory of my Dad

Paddy O'Brien
04-03-1919 - 03-12-2000

When I was small you held my hand,
I trusted and loved you till the end,
I lost two precious things on the December 3rd,
My father and my life long friend.

Mag x

Preface

There was something about my Dad. Actually there were many things about my Dad, which poses a dilemma as to where to start. My Dad, Paddy O'Brien, whom I sadly lost on December 3rd 2000 was one of the kindest, most patient, tolerant, deeply understanding and intuitive people I knew; not to speak of how lucky I was to have him as a Father. It is the calibre of the person that he was that inspired me to write about him. The poems which you will read in the following pages just came naturally as I started grieving for him. I have wanted to write a tribute to him for a long time and I thought that perhaps what I've written might help other people, by bringing them some measure of comfort while going through their grief for a Dad or Mum or any close person in their life. Just before each poem I will tell you a little about how it got started.

Acknowledgements

My thanks go first and foremost to my immediate care that did a champion job at getting me through my worst days. My husband Sean, for all your hugs, words of encouragement, advice, patience and most of all your love, your Mom would have been so proud of you.
My daughter Kerry, who adored her Granddad and he her, and was so sad herself. I thank you for your lovely warm hugs and your ability to smile and even joke, which got us through some very bad days. Stay your beautiful, scatty self.
My son Martin, who at the tender age of thirteen showed an acute understanding of my sadness, and would unprompted just open his arms and hold me, may you always be blessed, as you were then, with your Granddad's loving and intuitive heart.
To my many other family members and friends, for all their hugs, time to let me talk, in person or on the phone, flowers, cards, letters, money given without question, mass cards, prayers, companionable silences and distracting conversations depending on my mood that day. A gentle word on rough days, a hand salute or the tip of a working mans helmet, when I needed to be alone and any other gesture I may now have forgotten, you know who you are and you know what you did. Please know that my heartfelt thanks go to you all.

Mag.

Ode to my Dad Paddy O'Brien (R.I.P.)

This first poem came about on the eve of what would have been Dad's 82nd Birthday (my son Martin's 14th Birthday). Dad had passed on December 3rd 2000 after a long illness, and although we were sort of expecting it, you are never really ready. I was told on the phone by my sister Eileen at 10.30 on a Saturday night that he probably would not make it till morning. As you can imagine, it was with a heavy and sad heart that I went to bed that night. I normally slept through the night, but that night at 3.30am I awoke to what felt like a butterfly light tap on my shoulder. I noticed my bedside touch light was on and I distinctly remembered having tapped it off before falling asleep. Somehow, instinctively at that moment, I knew Daddy was gone. I believe he came to say goodbye, and that's what woke me. I looked across at my husband Sean sleeping soundly and realised he hadn't woken me; he was on his side of the bed, we were not touching. I laid my head back down and within minutes the phone rang. I instantly leapt over my sleeping husband and picked up the phone in the front room to hear my sister Eileen's tears as she tried to get the words out that Daddy was gone, but I already knew.

This was the first of many losses and shocks in the years to come, but that's another story. I had 41 years of a lovely friendship with my Dad and knew long before I could articulate it that he was special and that I was blessed to have had him as my Dad.

Ode to my Dad (Paddy O'Brien)

Was it really you, who came to me?
In the early morning, before dawn,
Tapped my shoulder and said "Goodbye",
So I would know you were really gone.

I really do believe it was you,
I felt your presence with me there,
It's the kind of thoughtful thing you'd do,
Just to let me know you cared.

The phone rang then, but I already knew,
That you had finally gone to rest,
One that was earned, well and true,
For Dad you always did your best.

You brought us up with love and care,
To be good to each other and others too,
Look out for each other and always share,
So many good things learned from you.

So Dad you'll know I miss you so,
From my life from day to day,
The loss is deep, God only knows,
Sometimes words just cannot say.

But I am lucky you were my Dad,
I've always known that to be true,
You were the best I could have had,
I was blessed to be loved by you.

So I'll carry your smile within my heart,

Your love in the crook of my arm,
And no matter how long we are apart,
I know you'll see I come to no harm.

03.03.01

Still missing you Dad

This poem like many of the others came out of the blue, no special day or date would bring them about. After speaking to others about their losses, I discovered how it affected them and how they dealt with their loss and grief. The person you have lost is on your mind virtually 24/7 in the first days and months and this is something we all had in common. By April 2001 I was going through those times, where I would get caught short by the enormity of my loss and sudden intense sadness would envelop me when I least expected it. For example, I would be walking in the street and see a broad built man of Irish appearance, big lonesome looking blue eyes, a kind face, a tweed cap turned slightly to one side and I would find myself crying softly in public. In itself, something I had never done before. On more than one occasion, I found myself crying in the aisles of Boots or Superdrug when I got a whiff of coal tar soap. For those of you who are not familiar with it, coal tar soap is wrapped in paper as opposed to plastic wrapping and has a strong pleasant male smell. (I call it.) My Dad always smelt of it as we used it a lot during my childhood for psoriasis.

I did not realise then of course (when I was crying in Boots or Superdrug) about the power of grief and the unique and individual ways it affects each and every one of us, but I have come to understand it since. So I was having one of those impromptu emotional days when this was written.

Still missing you Dad

Dad, I miss you so, since you went away,
I don't really know where I stand,
My life has changed a lot, in many different ways,
Without your love and your guiding hand.

No matter what I faced up until now,
You were always with me, like a guiding light,
Maybe not in person, but always in my soul,
And with you around, I usually got things right.

Now, I'm in a no-mans land,
It's a horrible place to be,
No one really understands,
How missing you makes me feel.

Now everything's changed around me,
I'm trying hard to make sense of it all,
I'm sure I will someday, you'll see,
But working it out without you is certainly not a ball.

But I know deep down, in my heart of hearts,
That all you taught me will stand me in good stead,
Your legacy is with me, though we're far apart,
My heart will mend and I'll get things straight in my
head.

24.04.01

Dad I miss your hugs

I wrote this poem on one of those days when I was actually missing my father physically, one of those days when I could really have done with one of his loving hugs. He was such an affectionate person. As young kids, (even after a long and I'm sure tiring days work for him) my siblings and I would jump on his lap and play hide and seek under his jacket. We would take his cap of his head and put it on each other (this was often with two or more of us vying for his attention), and he would accommodate us, never be short or irritable and always welcomed us with open arms. His 'guiding hand' referred to in my poem was the way he had about him, even when we were adults (and in my case, a parent myself), of instinctively knowing if something was the matter, be it physically or other wise. He always had the good grace to extract it out of us in our own good time and almost unknown to us. Then of course you'd feel a lot better and again tactfully and with much patience and love, he would try to help you get a handle on it. I sometimes wonder now, nearly seven years after his passing, if he realised what a good father he was to me and my siblings, or was that him just being him. Either way he had many good qualities which have helped me in my life as his daughter, and that has done me no harm in my later years as a mother and guide to my two children Kerry and Martin.

Dad I miss your hugs

I was told by someone I love dear,
You'd leave me something in your place,
I was too upset then, to really see clear,
But now I do, in a state of grace.

I know your spirit's still with me,
In a very special way,
I feel your presence around me,
In my life from day to day.

I never felt like this before,
It's hard to explain or say,
It affects me to my very core,
Good and sad on different days.

I know one thing to be really true,
No matter how much I miss you now,
My spirit is strong because of you,
Thanks for your gifts of grace and love.

I do understand you had to go,
Your time with us was done,
But I miss your hugs, and yourself more so,
Everything about you and then some.

06.05.01

Happy Father's Day Dad

Well, "Happy Father's Day Dad" speaks for itself I guess you'd say, and it does to a great degree. Although I stated in the preface that it did not have to be a special day or date to write something pertaining to my Dad, I assume you've gathered by now, that I was one of my Dads greatest fans. So, of course Father's Day brought words to mind. Armed with a pen in a quiet corner, those words ended up on paper yet again. It was becoming a bit of a habit, it was never planned, but the notion was on the back burner for a good few years. Something which reinforced it was a meeting on the night of my father's wake with a neighbour and old friend of his, Frank (a school teacher). We got talking about Dad and after exchanging our mutual appreciation for the man, he said, "You should write something about your father." Coming from a school teacher I took that as a compliment. So, now that I have finally got down to putting these thoughts in writing, perhaps I ought to take the time to say 'Thank You Frank for fuelling the fire of inspiration and enthusiasm.' This is probably a good time to explain that's what I meant in the preface by 'many things'. I know for a fact that many other friends and neighbours had good friendships and good times with my Dad, it's not just me. You could say okay, he was my Dad, but to them he could have been just another person, only he wasn't, because he was a people person. He genuinely liked people and made time for them and it would appear they did the same for him in return.

Happy Father's Day Dad

Dear Dad, Happy Father's Day to you,
You're first one away from me,
My saddest one yet, away from you,
The path without you is hard to see.

I am not angry, that you went away,
You really needed a good rest,
I am sad though, on some days,
But I do know, I had the best.

So this poem is a tribute to you,
To say with all my heart,
A great job done, God bless you,
Never forgotten, though we're far apart.

Enjoy your day, up there on high,
Thanks for the memories, left here with me,
You couldn't have done better if you tried,
In our ways, your legacy is plain to see.

16.06.01

Getting there slowly Dad

'Getting there slowly Dad' was quite literally what I was doing when this poem came out, about ten months on from losing Dad. For those of you in the early days of grief, crying a lot, not sleeping or eating a lot maybe, and often feeling very bereft, this time seems impossible to envisage. I myself felt the intensity of my loss as much and as hard to bear as the loss itself, if that makes sense. But, the human condition is an amazing and restorative one, and time actually does start to ease things some. Of course I am no expert nor do I claim to be, and I know that the fact that I both loved and liked my Dad very much and he me, probably made my grieving process for him that much more tolerable. There were no cross words, no regrets, just acute awareness that all the loose ends were tied up that last August. I had seen him in Ireland before he passed in December and I knew that summer that I would never see him alive again; don't ask me how, I just knew, and it saddened me immensely. I was cautious of saying anything to anyone about feeling like that, in case they might think I was crazy or that I was a bearer of doom, but I believe it was deeper and more spiritual than any of that. As soon as I knew that to be true and it came to pass, by the end of the first year, I also knew that I had all the good things he taught me to keep me going and keep me strong. Amazingly, they did and they do even to this day. I feel my Dad's spirit never left me, but instead cradles my shoulders like a warm shawl on a cool evening.

Getting there slowly Dad

Here I am again, and it's been a while,
Since I felt the need to write about you,
Life's gone on around me in its own style,
While I'm keeping busy, finding things to do.

You're often in my thoughts, and always in my
heart,
I talk about you often, in laughter and in tears,
Always, always remember though we're far apart,
Your name will pass my lips, often in coming years.

It makes me happy to talk about you,
And think of all the things you mean to me,
It's easy to recall, a man who was so true,
Made of strength, goodness, honour and dignity.

Your passing left my heart and soul,
Empty and sore beyond all say,
For others to have a Dads love,
Like yours for me, I can only pray.

They sure broke the mould, when they made you,
Your likes again, I will never see,
Look down on me, and I'll look up to you,
As life goes on, from sea to sea.

18.10.01

Many happy returns

Many happy returns, as this poem is so aptly named, was one of my Dad's favourite expressions on wishing us kids (and indeed anyone) celebrating a birthday good wishes, and his heart felt way of saying it, left you in no doubt of his sincerity. So needless to say on Father's Day and my birthday especially in that first year after his passing, those words rang clearly in my head and sat softly in the chambers of my heart. This birthday was a particularly poignant one for me, (although I had been acutely aware of it for years before his death) I realised how lucky I was to have had Paddy as my Dad. It was both a privilege and a blessing and I am certain that many of his morals and beliefs were directly or otherwise handed down to us children. In my own case, I know that a lot of these good things shaped the person I was eventually to become. I was unfortunate enough to have inherited psoriasis and eventually psoriatic arthritis from my Dad's bloodline, but as I've often told my children, I know these are not pleasant ailments, but if the choice was to be free of them and not have my Dad as my Dad, I'd choose them... Just to have him. He was the only person during my childhood to call me Mag and I loved it. I didn't like the name Margaret much, didn't mind Maggie or Mairead (My Irish name). Strangely enough since his passing my husband Sean calls me Mag and a few others too, and to hear it brings a quiet unseen smile to my heart.

Many happy returns

I woke up this morning and I thought of you,
It was a "Many Happy Returns" day for me,
My first one here in this world without you,
I'm so glad I had you for all the others you see.

I missed you a while, and shed some tears,
Then I thought of the things you used to say,
I thanked God that I had you for all those years,
And decided you'd want me to enjoy the day.

God Bless you always Dad, in your new place,
My bones are better, my heart a little lighter too,
I know I'll always see your lovely face,
And it's with pride and love, I'll think of you.

04.11.01

A year on

What can I say about a year on? A milestone, I got told at the time by a few people who had been where I was. Perhaps they were right, it took almost five years before the need to write about Dad arose again, as you'll see in the last poem. A year on was a confirmation of the fact that everything had changed forever. The first visit to our family home in Ireland, without Dad there, (the main figure in the house along with Mom of course) was a lonesome experience. The absence of his physical being in his chair at the head of the table, and the words you couldn't wait to hear on every visit as you neared the house "Welcome home a leanbh" (dear child), accompanied by a loving hug that left you in no doubt about how welcome you were, was palpable for me. I found myself going into his now almost empty room, and again that faint smell of coal tar soap, and the tears would come. Visiting his grave was very sad but also beneficial, because I lived in London. There were many times in that first year when I wished I could have, and if I could have it might have helped, I don't know. Yes, I suppose a year on was a kind of closure, although I sort of dislike that word. Dad will never be closed of from me and he's always with me in spirit. I derive great spiritual comfort from that, but it was a different kind of closure I guess, like natures way of making you understand the cycles of life. A person is born they live their life, leave their mark and pass on. You find ways to understand and accept all that with the loss of a parent, but it doesn't mean you forget them or the marks they left on you.

A year on

I've been home again to see you Dad,
A journey to help heal my heart,
The house without you was so sad,
The family together with you apart.

I missed your smile and your welcome home,
Shed some tears at your new resting place,
My heart felt low and so alone,
Knowing I'll never again see your face.

I wonder if others feel like me,
If someone has stolen a piece of their soul,
A special light's gone out of mine you see,
Not just any, you were made of solid gold.

I'll always love and miss you Dad,
From a place deep inside my heart,
I hope someday I won't feel so sad,
And with your guidance make a new start.

12.12.01

Hello Dad

"Hello Dad" was written on my Dad's 6th anniversary and on the heels of an impromptu weekend in Ireland, courtesy of my daughter Kerry and her partner Adam. Initially I was reluctant to go for two or three days but afterwards I was glad I did. An awful lot had happened since "A year on" in my life and in my family unit (Sean, Kerry and Martin). December 2002 I lost my youngest sister Bridie, we also lost quite a few members of Sean's family and some dear friends and neighbours too. Last but not least being the unspeakably tragic loss of Sean's nephew - his brother Peter's boy, Liam, 11 years old. So, we had been battered by so many losses and deeply shattered in their wakes and by the very fact that the losses kept coming. It was a very fragile me who visited my Dad and sister B's graves in November 2006. But it did my heart good to see my Mom, who was almost 85 years old, and to observe her during my visit. I took away with me the knowledge that no matter what losses my siblings and I had encountered in the previous few years (and we all had, in our various family units), Mom was just something else. If she could sit and entertain and visit and socialise at her age, we should learn from her. Life is precious, transient and lovely and hard and sad and many other things at different times, that's the nature of it. But it's not a dress rehearsal, so we must tell those we love or like, that we do love and or like them and do our best to cope with their loss, if they are called before us. To all those I loved and lost, and those you as a reader may have loved and lost, all that remains for me to say is, 'May they Rest in Peace until we meet again.'

Hello Dad

I awoke early this morning just before four am,
It was very wintry and the winds were high,
I soon remembered your time of passing was about the same,
How shockingly quickly those six years have gone by.

It's not that I'd forgotten you Dad,
Believe me that could never be,
It's hardly been three weeks back,
I visited again your grave and B's.

This time around I wasn't so lonely,
On visiting your joint resting place,
A kind of calmness has settled on me,
Acceptance I guess and I'm sure your grace.

Thanks again for the gifts you gave me,
They're standing up to the test of time,
Love, grace and of course dignity,
And it's thanks to you, that they're all mine.

03.12.06

GRAFFITI NOIR

By Suzannah Knight

Published by
Chipmunkapublishing
PO Box 6872
Brentwood
Essex CM13 1ZT
United Kingdom

http://www.chipmunkapublishing.com

Edited by Kimberley Bishop

1. MAXINE'S BEDROOM, AND OLD TOWN TERRACED HOUSE. DAY.

MAXINE *is a 25 year old, thin, blonde, beautiful, long haired woman, she is in her bedroom looking through an old jewellery box on her dressing table. The room is decorated with photos of Maxine on the walls. Maxine pulls a locket from the jewellery box and looks at it carefully. On the front is a coat of arms. She opens it up and inside is a picture of a young man and woman. The pictures are old and faded.*

TONY*, a forty five year old artist ragged with the face of an alcoholic and smoker, comes into the room. Maxine is putting on her chain and locket.*

TONY

Come on darling you must be ready by now.

MAXINE

Nearly, I'm just fixing my jewellery and makeup.

TONY

You look nice. Here let me help you with that... *(Tony whistles.)* Nice locket and chain. I bet that's worth a bob or two. We could pawn it to help out a bit.

MAXINE

No way it's the only thing I've got.

Maxine looks at a photograph of a woman on top of the mantelpiece and her face softens.

TONY *(Looks at the locket greedily.)*

It's a fancy coat of arms. Whose is it?

Maxine.

Never mind. Anyway aren't we in a hurry.

Tony fastens the necklace around Maxine's neck. When it falls the locket hangs below her low cut jumper unseen. Maxine applies some more lipstick. Tony is looking at his paintings.

TONY (CONT'D)

May as well burn thcm. Come on lets go to the pub.

They leave the room.

BLACKNESS.

FADE TO.

2. INT. THE TAVERN HOTEL DARLINGTON. NIGHT

The pub is quiet and seedy it is lit by red lamps in the windows. There are only one or two other drinkers in the pub. Tony and Maxine are sat at a table in the window drinking pints of lager. The door opens loudly and knocks the wall. Four drunken merry men walk in. ***STEINY****, a forty five year old distinguishable gentleman in a tweed suit is with three of his factory workers. Steiny notices Maxine and stares at her. Maxine also notices him, fancying him instantly. Steiny orders a drink at the bar. In a loud voice to one of his men he speaks.*

STEINY

Now that's what I call a fit woman.

Steiny grabs his drink and comes over to Tony and Maxine. He leans over the table, and reaches out his hand to shake with Tony.

STEINY (CONT'D)

Hello, I'm Steiny. I've never seen you in here before. Out with your daughter tonight?

Steiny sits down opposite Maxine. She looks down and takes a drink of beer.

TONY

She's not my daughter mate.

Maxine pulls a face and looks away annoyed.

MAXINE

Hi, I'm Maxine...And this is Tony, he's an artist.

STEINY

What sort of artist- a piss artist?

TONY

Very funny

STEINY

What are you then an art teacher or a painter and decorator?

TONY

I'm an out of work skint photographer. Why don't you go back to your factory colleagues?

STEINY

I own the furniture factory on Albert terrace.

TONY

Oh nice one.

Steiny looks at Maxine.

STEINY

Nice to meet you both.

Time passes by throughout the night and the glasses build up on the table. The bell goes for last time and Steiny, Maxine and Tony are all drunk.

Maxine gets up to go to the toilet. She smiles at Steiny as she passes him and takes her long hair out of it's ponytail and shakes her head.

Steiny orders two pints of lager and takes them over to Tony banging them down on the table.

STEINY

So does the photography keep that woman in luxury and expensive clothes?

TONY

Not at the moment, the photography world is a bit slow. I've been dumped by my bleeding agent to tell you the truth.

STEINY

Times are hard then are they?

TONY

That's not really any of your business.

STEINY

I could help you out you know.

TONY

Oh aye how?

STEINY

Maxine is a very beautiful woman. I'd be prepared to double what you make in the art business if you work at the factory. In return for something else of course.

TONY

Double it. In return for what?

Steiny takes a cigarette out of the packet and lights it, slowly inhaling deeply and exhaling deeply.

STEINY

Maxine.

TONY

Maxine. Oh no mate, she ain't like that.

STEINY

I'm not insinuating she is. Think about it, I'll make sure you're all right financially, it's not every day you get a chance like this, is it?

TONY

I'd like to knock you out.

Steiny gets up, he hands Tony a business card, and returns to the bar. Maxine returns and sits down.

TONY

Drink up I want to go. That Steiny is beginning to get on my nerves.

MAXINE

He seems all right.

TONY

He will be when I've laid him out.

BLACKNESS.

FADE TO.

3. int. Tony AND MAXINE'S LIVING ROOM. DAY.

Maxine is eating some biscuits. The clock reads 10.30 am. The room is small but quite lavish, apart from the old carpet which is black and dirty. Tony walks in. He gets a can of beer out of the drinks cupboard. There is a photography stand in the corner, Tony takes his fists and feet and smashes it to the ground in a rage. Maxine flinches and then stares out of the window looking miserable, rain is falling heavily. Tony lights a cigarette, and inhales deeply. Tony looks around the room walls drinking in all the nude paintings of Maxine in erotic poses. Laid on the table are a pile of unpaid bills.

MAXINE

What's wrong with you?

TONY

Nothing.

Tony finishes his can and crumples it. He cracks open another.

TONY

Want a beer sweetheart?

Tony cracks open a can for Maxine.

MAXINE

Its ten thirty in the morning Tony, you shouldn't be drinking.

TONY

There's more nutrition in this can of beer than in any of the food in this house.

MAXINE

Go on then. Come on tell me what's on your mind. I know something's up.

TONY

That fucking job offer from that Steiny, I told you about it last night.

MAXINE

I would have thought you would have accepted that there and then, but then it was a bit weird. But hey, don't look a gift horse in the mouth and it was kind in a way.

TONY

Yeah really fucking kind. Listen, I wasn't going to tell you, but the geezer wants to pay me double my salary in exchange for shagging you.

MAXINE

What? What are you talking about?

TONY

I'm saying he wants me to pimp you.

MAXINE

And would you?

TONY

Course I wouldn't but...

MAXINE

But what? You're thinking about it, is that it Tony?

TONY

You wouldn't mind would you cos you fancy him don't you? I saw you looking at him. Well now you can shag him and make some money. Which makes all this and us a load of bullshit.

Tony gets up in a rage and smashes up the pictures of Maxine on the walls, wrecking the place. Maxine cowers in the corner on the settee. Tony sits back down putting his head in his hands.

MAXINE

Tony you're scaring me.

TONY

I'm scaring myself sweetheart.

MAXINE

You mean I'm going to be a lady of the night, a hooker for that rich bastard. Does he think he can just buy people? And you, you think you can sell me!

TONY

What the fuck am I going to do? I'm not going to get any other work around here.

MAXINE

I am not a prostitute.

TONY

Listen you lazy cow why don't you go out and get a job yourself... The money would buy you fancy clothes and makeup. We could do up the house, new flooring... Think about it Maxine. He's offering us double what I make doing the art.

MAXINE

Jesus Tony, you're asking me to whore for your boss. It's a bit weird isn't it? I mean who the fuck propositions people like that?

TONY

Robert Redford. Rich geezers like that Maxine think they can do anything they want. It's called money sweetheart and we'd have plenty of it if…

MAXINE

No way Tony.

Tony looks furious. He holds his fist to Maxine's face.

TONY

You'll get this if you don't...

FADE TO.

4. Int. The tavern hotel bedroom, DARLINGTON. NIGHT.

Maxine enters the hotel bedroom. The hotel room is tatty and dressed in 1960's faded materials and furniture. Steiny is stood at the dressing table. He looks up and smiles as she walks towards him. She looks down shyly.

STEINY

I didn't think you'd come, but it's very nice to see you.

Steiny leans forwards and kisses her on the cheek.

Would you like some tequila? A double?

Maxine smiles. Steiny pours a large glass of the amber liquid.

STEINY (CONT'D)

I'm glad you came, clever girl. What is a very beautiful girl like you doing with that idiot?

MAXINE

Tony's alright really, it's a long story you wouldn't be interested.

STEINY

Yes I would.

MAXINE

I'd rather not.

STEINY

I'll have heard worse.

MAXINE

Well my mum died nine years ago... And left me destitute. I had nothing... And

STEINY

And then you met Tony.

MAXINE

Yeah I met Tony and started posing nude for photographs. People everywhere have seen them, so I keep myself locked away from life in his house. I've never been brave enough to leave.

STEINY

Lots of women have taken their clothes off. Always have always will.

MAXINE

Are you married?

STEINY

Yes

Maxine looks upset.

MAXINE

Thought you were. Damn.

STEINY

What about your father?

MAXINE

Oh that's always been a touchy subject.

STEINY

Why?

Steiny pours another drink. Maxine moves over to the bed and sits down on it.

MAXINE

Oh my father left my mother before I was born, she wasn't from the right class if you know what I mean. That's what she always said anyway.

STEINY

Why don't you come and live with me. I have an apartment in Waddingham Castle and I'd like it if you lived there. My wife and I have an arrangement you see. She's badly disabled now...

MAXINE

I'll think about it.

Maxine is now lying on the bed in her underwear and stockings. Steiny's eyes nearly pop out of his head. He stares at Maxine's body and then goes over to her.

STEINY

Have you ever been loved before?

MAXINE

No.

STEINY

Then I'll show you how.

FADE TO:

Maxine and Steiny are in bed, kissing. Steiny is laying on top of Maxine. He rolls off her and they hug both falling asleep.

FADE TO

The window is open and the white voile is blowing in the wind. Maxine wakes up. On the bedside table is Steiny's wallet and signet ring. Maxine checks Steiny is asleep and opens his wallet. She finds a thousand pounds in cash and takes hold of it. Slowly thinking she puts it back. Maxine turns to Steiny and looks at him affectionately. Then she picks up the ring examining it. Looking at the coat of arms carefully she takes her locket and compares them. They are exactly the same. She then looks at the photo of her father and realizes it could be a very young Steiny. Maxine throws the locket and ring at Steiny with a stricken face. Steiny stirs and awakes.

THROUGH THE EYES OF A MANIC

By
Lesley Watson

Chipmunka Anthology Volume Six

Published by
Chipmunkapublishing
PO Box 6872
Brentwood
Essex CM13 1ZT
United Kingdom

http://www.chipmunkapublishing.com

Edited by Caroline Mansi

Introduction

Many people have a fear of the unknown; mental illness defiantly falls into this category. The fear of what the person is going to do next, as they are highly erratic and unpredictable. But people must remember there is a person inside there somewhere who is probably even more scared than you are. Its human nature to lash out and struggle when you are scared, yet police are often called to help with mental illness and the way they handle the situation makes matters worse. They seem to fight fire with fire. There is much discrimination against people with mental health problems. All the people I have met who suffer from manic episodes have, at some time, suffered abuse in the past or experienced a great trauma. Instead of just drugging people up until the next time they can't cope it's about time people started to listen and try to understand WHY. This is my experience ……

I was born in the north of England. I have an older sister; Tereasa and a younger brother; Jason. I had lived in the north England for nine years, although we moved around a lot with my father's job.

My father was a very strict man and was a devoted catholic. Every Sunday all three children would put on their Sunday bests and attend church. My memory of church is; if I was naughty my father would march me to the outside of the church and smack me, not beat me but a small smack to teach me discipline. The same would happen to Tereasa and Jason if they misbehaved. My mother was a lovely woman. She worked hard keeping the house in order; washing, ironing and taking care of her three adorable children. My mum and dad loved each other dearly, they never argued or drank alcohol and my dad worked very hard to give his wife and children the best he could.

I was happy living up north but my dad was reposted and we had to move to the south. I was nine years old when we moved.

At first I found it difficult to adjust to my new school but it didn't take long before I made new friends. The head master of the school would walk around using his fist to 'knuckle head' the boys on the head, I was terrified of him. There was one time when me and one of my friends were called to his office, we had fallen out with another girl and were being nasty to her, but when we went to the headmaster's office we didn't expect to be threatened with the cane. I stood there knees and legs uncontrollably shaking. Although I knew what we had done was wrong, I thought being told off by the headmaster would have been enough to put the fear of god into me, but he stood there hitting the cane on the desk. It was a sight I would never forget and would have nightmares of him vigorously slamming it down.

My sister was very intelligent; she passed all of her exams so the government would pay for her to go to private school. This gave her a step in the right direction. I, however, was more of a daydreamer; I was just as clever but didn't follow in her footsteps.

My real problems began when I attended secondary school. It was a catholic school twenty miles away from where I lived. I was quiet and petite which made me an immediate a target for the bullies. I was teased day in and day out, pushed, nudged and tripped over. Because of this I began to skip off school. One day whilst wondering around I met a girl a year younger than myself, her name was Louise.

Louise had a northern accent and it turned out that she was from the same town as me. We became really close friends and Louise introduced me to many girls and boys. I began going out all the time hanging around with Louise and a group of older boys. My parents were not happy about this but me and Louise became inseparable.

There was one lad that I really liked, his name was Paul and he was 16. One night he invited Louise and me back to his friend's house. John, Paul's friend, had the house to himself as his parents had gone on holiday.

It was September and the nights drew in early. Louise and I both had to be in by nine but it was still quite early so we decided to go.

Louise left the house in plenty of time to get home but as I only lived a couple of mins away I decided to stay a little longer. As soon as Louise had left Paul took hold of my hand and led me upstairs. I was thirteen years old had an innocent mind and body. Paul led me straight into the bathroom as it had a lock on it. At the time I didn't panic as my probity didn't register what he intended to do. That night my whole life fell apart.

Once in the bathroom, he locked the door and started to insert one, two and more fingers inside of me. I screamed "no stop you're hurting me". Tears of pain ran down my face but this seemed to excite him more. As I yelled for him to stop I heard John giggling at the door. After what seemed to be forever he casually removed his blooded hand, ran the tap and washed the blood off. I thought that it was all over and tried to pull up my knickers but as I did so he stopped me and began to kiss my privates. I froze in panic and despair as he performed oral sex on me. All I felt was pain, humiliation, shame and mortification. Tears rolled down my face silently, no sobs or screams. I wiped my tears and collapsed in an emotional mess as he satisfied himself.

In a trance I walked down stairs, headed for a bottle of vodka and began drinking it like water as the two boys giggled like little girls. I had never drunk alcohol before so it didn't take long for the effects to take hold. John started to worry as he knew I was meant to be home, so the pair of them decided to sober me up. Paul went upstairs and ran a bath of cold water; they carried me upstairs and threw me in with my clothes on. The next thing I knew they were taking my clothes off to put them in the tumble dryer, it was way past the time I was supposed to be in and they knew somehow they had to get me home. I stood in the kitchen drunk, naked, ashamed, and humiliated I felt totally lost. While they were tumble drying my clothes they threw me in the back garden without a stitch on. I became hysterical screaming "Paul why did you do this to me". I sat curled up in the garden with blood trickling down my legs.

Although my clothes were still damp it was about half past ten so John dressed me and started to carry me home. As we got down the road he saw some friends of his who had a car and they offered to help him to get me home.

When I arrived home my dad answered the door, he was devastated to see me in such a drunken state and couldn't thank John enough for bringing me home safely.

Once indoors I was carted upstairs and reprimanded for coming home late and in such a state. "What will the neighbors think?" I laid in my room screaming at them "He split me, he split me". I kept screaming it at them but whether they didn't understand what I was saying or were just to ashamed of me I will never know but they didn't take any notice. My sister was trying to make me sick to sober me up by giving me warm salt water to drink as I screamed to her what had happened. Their main concern seemed to be to sober me up. The more they ignored me the more hysterical I became, repeating over and over what he had done but my cries were in vain as they weren't listening to me.

The following morning was so strange, it was as though nothing had happened, and no one mentioned anything. There was blood on my sheets but my mum just assumed that I was having a period. My whole life had just crumpled apart. From then on my heart was pumping pain through my veins. My sister didn't even question anything. They must have been so ashamed of me! Although I was very drunk the memories of that night are as clear as a whistle.

I had lost faith in everything; in my parents, in my sister and most of all in God. If there was a god why did this happen to me? Yet every Sunday I still had to go to church. I would put my fingers down my throat to make myself sick so I didn't have to go but I had no choice.

This was my turning point. I shaved my hair, stuck it up with gel and pierced my own ears and nose. On the outside I was as hard as nails, I pushed the girl that bullied me down the stairs at school and then I became the bully. I wasn't going to let anyone hurt me again but I was totally destroyed on the inside.

There was only one person I could talk to about what had happened and that was Louise but because of the incident my parents didn't like me associating with her. I love my parents and family but despise them at the same time, they put my rebelling down to teenage hormones, however, my rebellious attitude was fuelled with anger, frustration and aversion.

Some people who suffered abuse feel the need to clean themselves, nevertheless I was left so distressed I went totally the opposite way. I felt so dirty I never washed. I lost all respect and love for my self.

I also rebelled against god, one day I found a key in the church. It didn't take me long to discover that it belonged to the collection box. The church was unlocked most of the time so I would steal money from the church to buy cigarettes. I gave my virginity away at a young age and disrespected my body. Through all the anguish I never turned to drink or drugs to help me deal with it. I found a lot of comfort in listening to music.

When I was sixteen I met a man called Jamie. When I introduced him to my parents they both immediately disliked him this obviously made me see more of him and after being with him for six months we got engaged. This really upset my parents, however, they did say that if I was happy then so were they.

On my eighteenth birthday things went wrong. I wanted to go out and celebrate my birthday but Jamie wanted to stay in and watch a dirty movie and then have sex. We argued and it got out of control, so much that he put his hand around my neck which made me physically sick. He then punched me so hard in the face that my cheek bone was chipped. A few days later he took me to the hospital, the nurses there must have thought he was a relative. As when I explained what had happened they asked me while he was standing there, if I wanted to prosecute my fiancée. I should have learnt by this. But in October 1988 I married him.

Shortly after I discovered that I was pregnant. At last I was going to have someone all of my own to love dearly. I was sure of my dates as my birthday is in November and I had been to the doctors to confirm my pregnancy. Which means my baby would be due July time. My pregnancy went fine with no problems.

My due date came and went, two weeks had gone by and I was becoming anxious and rather tired when at last I had a sign, I thought my waters had gone. I became very scared of the unknown pain as every first time mother is. Some of the stories you here are rather frightening. I rang the hospital and was told to come in to have a check over. Excited and full of fear I picked up my case, which had been standing in the hallway for over a month, and headed to the maternity ward at the local hospital.

On arrival I was shown to a side room and asked to wait until the doctor was available. When he arrived there were no tests done, he just looked and told me that my waters were still intact. I was then told to return home and wait, I tried to explain to him that I was two weeks over my due date but he insisted that I go home and return on the 25 August unless I started to get any discomfort or pain. I was upset and disappointed and emotionally I had had enough of this pregnancy.

By 25 August I still was carrying my baby but this time I knew my little one would be with me soon. My stomach was churning with anticipation excitement but most of all I was petrified. I was immediately taken to the labor ward and put onto a drip with in two minutes the contractions began; the baby's heartbeat was monitored and then I was just left. I was mortified, all my fears began to surround me. After what seemed to be hours of pain it all got too much for me the pain was unbearable. I had a hand button so I pressed it to receive help. When she arrived in the room she was very abrupt and snapped at me "What do you want?" Shocked and stunned at this I asked for some gas and air to help with the pain "it's over there!" was the reply I received, then, with the same ill manner that she had when she came in, she left the room. My husband had to get it for me and it seemed to help a little, then suddenly the monitor, which was keeping an eye on the baby's heart, started to bleep loudly this obviously startled me and I began to panic, calling for the midwife again. This time she was worse than before, she didn't seem to have any concern for my feelings nor the care of my baby. "What do you want now" I explained what had happened but she just walked off, saying "that's nothing"

I was devastated, I felt trapped, fearful and also I was in great pain but no way was I going to ask for help, I was terrified to do so. After what seemed like eternity the door opened again and a group of people walked in (there were about five doctors). No one introduced themselves, yet they were talking to each other. I was made to feel like an object not a human being. Then, without anything being explained to me the female consultant gave me an internal. As she did so, I had a terrible, sharp pain in my cervix and I screamed exclaiming how much it hurt. "Of course it would your having a baby" she made feel so small, it was if she was mocking me. Then she carried on talking to the other people in the room as if I wasn't even there. "She should be at least three centimeters by now, but she is only one".. You can imagine the thoughts going through my head, I was wondering if there was anything wrong with me! By that time, all I wanted to do was to go home. The next thing I can remember I was being rushed to theatre for an emergency caesarean.

I woke up early hours of the morning to the sound of babies crying, I looked around for my baby to hold him for the first time but there was no crib at my bedside. In a panic I tried to move but it was too painful, I called for the nurse. When she got to me I was in a state, asking where my baby was. She calmed me down telling me he was fine but that he was in the special care unit for the time being because he wasn't feeding properly. I hadn't seen him or held but he was whisked away from me just because he wasn't feeding properly? All this didn't make any sense to me, something wasn't right! He was only hours old, why had they got him in special care? I hadn't even seen him! Still I turned over and went tried to sleep with the noise of other babies crying in the background.

The next morning I woke up on a ward, all the other new mothers were walking around holding caressing and nursing their babies. I really wanted to nurse my new baby and watching other mothers made me feel empty, lonely and extremely isolated. Mind you, my feelings were considered, as on my bedside cabinet there was a Polaroid photo of my son. Mind you I don't know weather this made me feel better at all as I had to lay there surrounded by new mums with their babies; bonding, holding and feeding them when I was left holding a Polaroid photo. I just wanted to be with my son and I wanted him to be with me.

I was taken to see my son in a wheel chair as I peered into the cot I saw the most beautiful the most gorgeous little baby boy he was perfect! I held him close and tried to nurse him but he had a tube fitted through his nose and he wasn't interested. I felt terribly rejected by this but it was explained to me that he was being fed through this tube! Deep inside I felt something wasn't right.

Three days later my sister had come to visit me and while she was there a nurse wheel my son into the ward. My heart started to beat faster (at last I would have him with me!) He was handed to me and I held him close and fed him. He fed well for ten minutes but straight after, the nurse took him back. I was devastated, all my dreams were being shattered, all I wanted was to be with my little one to bond and love him. I was told he was only brought to me to see if he would feed properly.

The next time I went to S.C.B.U I burst into tears, emotionally I had had enough. I explained to the nurse how I was feeling. To my surprise she responded to my distress by saying coldly "there are people worse of than you!" By this time I had had enough, all I wanted to do was to go home with my baby, I was sick of being treated like dirt.

After five long days of hell, watching other mothers bonding with their new ones, my son was brought to me to stay. Shortly after, I went down stairs and out the front for a cigarette (by now my hormones started to kick in with revenge). As I was smoking, at first it felt as if it was my first fag for a long time, I felt kind of dizzy and light headed but the feeling of being light headed became stronger and stronger with each drag of the cigarette, I had no control over this. It was very freighting, as I had no control over these feelings and I was getting higher and higher, not pleasurable but very scary. All of a sudden I felt a tremendous force pulling me towards my baby. It's difficult to explain, it was like it was like a feeling of great need to bond (he needed me just as much as I needed him). I ran up the stairs screaming "I am coming" but something inside me was telling me to slow down and don't run! So I slowed down fighting this great yearning to get to my baby. The closer I got to him the stronger this strong emotion became, the need to hold, the need to bond, this overwhelming feeling of love ran through every vain in my body pumping faster and faster (God knows what would have happened if I had ran hysterically to him, which is what I wanted to do). As I approached him, hormones had sent me higher than the clouds, but reaching out to him and holding my babe close I slowly came down and back to earth; he calmed me down and stopped all these terrifying feelings! I was now totally determined to go home and take my precious son home with me. So when the doctor came I told her. At first she wasn't happy to send me home but I was adamant so she discharged me.

My mum came to collect us and took us home. As we were driving away from the hospital I started to go high again but this time was different, I felt great. Fantastic. This feeling was of tremendous joy; I was getting out of that ghastly place.

On arriving home, my baby needed feeding I took him into the bedroom and nursed him. For the first time it was just me and him, it was the moment I will always cherish, as he suckled from me he received pure love and just by accepting I received that love back (he was feeding fine, why had they lied to me?)

After this,, the computer inside my head went into speed mode sending hormones and searching for an answer. The hormones took me off this planet and into a terrifying dimension… I began to pace up and down the landing puffing and panting hysterically, trying to make scene but unable to speak. I was experiencing a massive panic attack this was a fearful experience. I had to get out of the flat, so my husband and I wrapped the baby up and went for a walk. My husband knew there was something wrong but nothing could prepare anyone for what was about to happen.

We didn't get very far (just outside the family church) when suddenly all my sanity was taken away I had a massive anxiety attack. It was twice as frightening. It felt as though the ground was opening up and pulling me down, down, down with great force. I took a deep breath and screamed from the very depth of my soul, "HELP, HELP". I was outside his house pleading him for help (but no one could help me now, I was about to begin a ten year sentence of hell). One of the neighbors had heard the commotion and invited us in their house while my husband called for help. My mum and doctor were called. I was scared, no, petrified; I could not communicate with anybody. I was in this world in body, but in my mind, my brain had taken over and it was working overtime at the speed of light. Something terrible had happened to my baby and me (my mind would not let go of this until someone would listen and perhaps understand).

The doctor advised that I go to the hospital so my mum took me in the car. On the way there I was violently pushing my breasts (if my baby didn't want them neither did I). My nightmare was just beginning and already was getting worse, I was being taken back to the one place I fought so hard to get away from. As I walked through the doors at the casualty apartment I couldn't breath, I was fighting for every breath I took, panic filled the air around me. "She must have had a traumatic time during labour, she is reliving the birth". This wasn't what I was experiencing but I was so out of this world in a frightening dimension that I couldn't talk or communicate with anyone around me.

I was immediately taken to the psychiatric ward and placed in a side room. As the psychiatrist came into the room with several other nurses my mind did a wiz back to the labour room, I curled up into a little ball, saying "don't touch me please don't hurt me!" I was repeating these words in a hysterical manner. Then I noticed one of the nurses had long black hair similar to the doctor who humiliated me during my labour, she was wearing a red top. I then became more disturbed pointing to her screaming "lady in red, lady in red". I was in a horrifying dimension, all the doctors saw was a hysterical psychotic woman, yet I was a very scared individual whose mind would not stop until someone would listen. For almost a month night and day I would wet the bed, scream that my waters had gone, then go totally mad screaming, "they have taken my baby" over and over again. I didn't slow down and sleep for this period of time. The doctors tried ever drug on market to slow my brain down, I was seriously in a very psychotic state of mind. Nothing worked; my will was too strong, drugs weren't going to stop this pain inside! The doctor told my mother that it was like a huge heart attack in the brain and if they couldn't slow it down my brain would eventually wear my body out and I would die. The last resort was electric shock treatment.

My father, being the religious man he was decided to take me to the little chapel, as I walked in the atmosphere was breathtaking; the whole chapel was full with love. At first it was frightening but as this feeling became stronger it became more beautiful than you could ever imagine. I turned to my father and said, “Dad, he is here, I can feel him!” he said I was overreacting and of course he's here it was his house. I felt the presence of a wonderful being that day; he had answered my screams for help. I believe I was, that day, blessed by the hands of God!

I was given E.C.T and at last I began to slow down, but as I did so the medication started to work this left me walking around like a zombie, still refusing to sleep, scraping my feet along the floor and dribbling from the mouth. I looked like someone from a horror movie but inside I was a human being. Eventually I slept and I was on the mend. The whole experience was too traumatic for me and my mind blocked all memory of the whole ordeal.

Before I was discharged from the unit the psychiatrists decided that it would be helpful if my husband came into the unit and stay as a family. I was still on a lot of drugs and heavily sedated on haloparadol, procicligen, timazipan and other sedatives, yet when my husband arrived he was handed a hand full of condoms to prevent further pregnancy. As I was so heavily sedated I would go in to a deep sedated sleep. Although I can understand this precaution, it gave my husband some kind of perverted pleasure in having sex with me whilst I was asleep. I would wake up in the morning to find a used condom on the floor! This sick behavior carried on for many years through our marriage.

I didn't want sex with him at all and refused him when he asked. This made no difference to him, as he would wait until I was asleep. As I came off my medication I began to wake up when he was touching me, on one occasion I recall waking up finding he had his head between my legs. I had told him about my past and he knew how I felt, at times I would lay there silently crying, with tears rolling down my face hoping and praying he would finish soon. But whom could I tell? I had no friends, he made sure of that.

In 1990 I fell pregnant with my second child. Myself and the family were obviously apprehensive, as the odds of my illness happening again were very high. I had a social worker and I told them that I couldn't cope with my husband's sexual needs. I was about 27 weeks pregnant. My being pregnant didn't stop him from fulfilling his sexual activity. As before, my pregnancy went well. I went to the same hospital and things were different this time, the nurse didn't leave the room and I was given an epidural. On 1st June I gave birth to a beautiful baby girl.

It was when I got home things went wrong. My husband lost his job and I suppose a week was too long for him to go with out sex, I woke up to him touching me and trying to enter me! I still had stitches in and found this extremely painful. All memories of my last psychosis started to come flooding back, fear ran through my veins again. Scared and not knowing what to do I took my new born and phoned a taxi to go to my mothers. When I arrived at my mums she was not impressed, it was the early hours of the morning and she couldn't understand why I needed to talk to her. I told her what he had done, I felt so dirty. I began to clean my mums house (this made sense to me, as that man had made me feel so unclean and dirty I felt I had to clean things) yet with this and the memories of what happened after my son, my soul and my emotions couldn't cope, I needed help. So I went back to the psychiatric ward.

I went there voluntarily but when I arrived and walked through the doors my heart started pounding with fear. The fear of what had gone on there back in 1989 rushed through me the memories were as clear as if it had happened yesterday. I wanted to tell how clear things were in my mind but all they were interested in was to get medication into my system, as they were fearful I was going psychotic. Then without warning several nurses grabbed me by my arms and legs all my body weight was on my shoulders and the physical pain in them was horrendous. At one point the doors were closed and they squeezed me passed as I screamed in pain for them to stop, it felt as though my arms were being ripped of at the shoulders. I felt that there was no need for this kind of violence towards me!

Once I was in a room a doctor came, I was begging him not to give me any medication as I knew it would stop me from feeding my baby, "you took that away from me last time please don't do it again" I asked, the doctor seemed very concerned and he actually showed some human emotion; he had tears in his eyes listening to my pleas but still he had to gave me a large dose of a sedative. I was out like a light. I slept solid for three days, three days of darkness, no dreams, just pure blackness. All I wanted to do was to let these feelings, these memories of 1989 out. There was one nurse who had been there in 1989 and he was very supportive. He let me go in the room were I was then and explain to him what I was feeling. This helped me tremendously as he listened and confirmed everything I was remembering. I was scared as my feelings were taking over but this nurse was a blessing to me. Since I was in the ward last they had built a mother and baby unit so my baby was able to come into the hospital with me. It wasn't long before I was well enough to go home. It was around four weeks before I was discharged, still on a lot of drugs I was sent back to that scum of a man, much to his sexual delight!! He would also keep me in like a prisoner, if I went to the shops he would time me and if I were longer than ten minutes he would be verbally violent to me. If we were out shopping in Sainsbury's I learned to keep my eyes to the ground because if I looked at another man the shopping trolley would be rammed into the back of my legs. I was trapped in a world of abuse.

Years went by, years of being interfered with. Every time I mentioned what he was doing there was disbelief, as by the time I was able to tell someone, the emotional pain, the feeling of being nothing and my mental state of mind had deteriorated. My life was hell on earth, no way out but to carry on letting him abuse me. His sexual actions were not normal, he used to sit up in the loft of our home with his air rifle and he would use the center of a dirty magazine as a target! It should have been him seeing a Psychiatrist not me!!

Then one night we had got a couple of young girls to baby-sit for us, we didn't often go out so we took the opportunity. When we returned the baby sitters looked concerned and worried, and not until my husband had gone to bed did they tell me what was troubling them. While we were out my little girl, who was then two years old, told them quiet innocently that daddy had made my Marie-Anne happy. He was destroying my life and now my whole world crashed down on top of me. I was devastated and fearful for her, I knew what he was doing to me and I believed he was capable of touching my little girl.

I couldn't cope with this, I told mum my fears and again what he was doing to me; I wasn't emotionally strong enough to hold on to my sanity. There was disbelief, my mother and family had associated my accusations of sexual activity as a sign of my illness and emotionally in my mind I went back to 1989 like I did every time before I broke down. Yet again back to the psychiatric ward, drugged up, no one listening, no one caring, E.C.T to bring me back to earth, then again placed back, all drugged and ready for another round of being shagged while I was asleep by that evil perverted man.

I saw a psychiatrist regularly but every time I tried to talk about 1989 or my abuse I was told not to talk about, as I would be ill.

Three years after 1989 I wrote a complaint to the hospital, I did this with the help of my C.P.N who was very helpful. I then received a letter of reply saying that the reason my baby was in special care was because my WATERS HAD GONE, by this time I couldn't do anything about the situation but the jigsaw in my head started to make sense. Unfortunately my mental health record was so strong that who the hell would believe me? Everything fell into place but no one would listen to me as they were scared that I was ill and I was forever been told 'don't talk about it' 'leave it in the past' but my mind wouldn't let me!!!

At some point in 1994 I plucked up the courage to tell the family doctor (I felt that he might help me out of this dreadful situation). I told him how I was feeling abused by my husband when he touched me in my sleep, to my surprise he began to laugh at me saying that some women enjoy that. At this reaction from him I began to cry, as it was clear that I didn't enjoy it. He then began saying that he was worried about me as I was a manic-depressive and I was very distressed. I still wasn't strong enough to stand up to the doctors, not on my own with no support. My faith in the community and the mental health team was lost completely; the only help I ever received was drugs, which only helped temporarily by pushing the main problem to the back of my mind until it returned again.

When my daughter was four years old we I was giving her a bath when she presented her private parts to me. She was very red and sore. When she got out of the bath she walked straight out the bathroom and into my room and took one of her dads' dirty magazines. She opened it up and then put her hand between her legs; these kind of actions from a four year old in my opinion is not normal behavior. I took the magazine and gave her a hug, immediately I remembered what she had said to the baby sitters. My heart sank. The next morning I rang social services and explained to them everything, I was quite distraught, beginning with the fact that my husband was abusing me physically mentally and sexually. I then went on to tell them what I thought he was doing to my daughter. Unfortunately my illness took hold of my emotions but at least I had told someone who would listen to me!! But then again when I was discharged from the hospital nothing had changed and nothing had happened.

Shortly after my release from the hospital my husband eventually gave me a way out of my marriage, he told me that he had got a seventeen girl pregnant - he was twenty-seven!! This was a relief to me but he then started to deny being the child's father. After seven years of marriage in January 15th 1996 I received my decree absolute!!

Although I was out of that awful marriage he had left me with little no absolutely no self-respect. My house was always messy and I was out to hurt men as much as they had hurt me! I was left a very lonely women with two young children (who hardly saw him as he lost interest after a while) who could only wallow in self pity and live in the past of abuse and shame!! My children were always loved, kept clean and fed well. My ambition to hurt men was to no avail. It never made me feel any better and all along I was the one getting hurt. And how can you hurt men who are only after one thing? I had made myself a target for more abuse.

I felt life as a single mother was hard and I was very lonely. I was scared of being alone in this world. My neighbour on one side took great offence in having a single mum who was a manic depressive living next door to her. She did everything in her power to make my life hell, for instance when my husband first left she started complaining to the police about the slightest noise. I would play my music at what I thought was a reasonable level, yet I received a visit from the local police officer. When he arrived I invited him in and showed him the volume that I was playing my music on. He responded to me by saying he thought that that was reasonable after going next door and checking the noise levels. So I carried on play music at that level yet several weeks later I was summoned to the council offices and received a warning about my music. The police had supported her claims, which confused me as every time the police arrived on my door due to calls from my neighbor I was assured by them that my music was not load enough to cause any disturbance to my neighbour.

As I felt so lonely I would invite the wrong kind of company into my house. I started a relationship with a man I had known when I was a teenager, he was not the ideal man for me and my family, but thinking so little of myself I didn't set my standards very high. I felt that I didn't deserve anything better. I had put myself so low I couldn't get any lower, with the police coming round about noise and my so called boyfriend going out all night with other women I was still having breakdowns.

At one time I was arrested by the police as I was so high due to my illness. They treated me as though I was on drugs, threw me into the cells and psychically attacked me. They were fully aware of my illness yet their response to my calls for assistance was appalling.

While I was in hospital I needed someone to look after the family dog, so my mum gave my keys to my younger brother to feed and walk her. During this time at my house my brother took round his amplifier and boosted the music out at loud decibels! This gave the neighbour the ideal opportunity to call the environmental health. This resulted in a noise abatement order. When I was well again I got rid of my stereo so all I had in the house was a clock radio, but even then she still banged on the walls and the police still would turn up!

After a long period of time I confronted her and her boyfriend, this didn't go very well as I ended up lashing out at him, causing her to attack me and in self-defense I grabbed her hair. Fifteen minuets later an ambulance appeared and she was taken to hospital, she had bruises all over her back and also she had to wear a neck brace. I can assure you I did not afflict those injuries upon her! One week later I was arrested for actual body harm, the police took my statement and I was bailed pending investigation. This time my neighbour made several mistakes with her statements, at first her boyfriend was a passer by, which made him an independent witness, then when the police visited her again he was present and this time he was her boyfriend, then he was her husband. So her statements didn't add up. I was charged with common assault and received a caution. They were determined to get me evicted. There was one person who believed every complaint she received and this was the housing officer. Because of the noise order on the house I was issued with an eviction notice.

After a long time with this drug addict our relationship ended. The only problem was because I had got to know his friends my house was still open to all the waif and strays. I welcomed a young man who had just got out of prison. He was on heavy drugs and had nowhere to live, he was only 17 and I was 27. I began a relationship with him, although it wasn't serious.

In 1998 my dad died. He was very ill for a while and it was expected, even so I was devastated. That evening I went to bed early as I was feeling very upset, when this young man arrived back he had been taking a lot of drugs, he had other ideas he wanted to have sex. I told him to leave me alone but he just kept on and on, all I wanted was someone to hold and make me feel safe but all he wanted was sex. I begged him to stop, but he went on and on till four in the morning I eventually gave up and gave him what he wanted!!

When I woke up the next morning I asked him to leave, he refused to do so. A friend of mine came round and managed to get the keys of him and he left.

I was so distraught I didn't want to stay in the house that night so I took my two children and stayed at a friend's house. While I was out he returned to my house, he must have broken in to find I wasn't there. He lost his temper and started kicking the walls; the neighbours didn't call the police. I came back home to find him in my house. I ran to a friend's house and called the police. By this time I was an emotional wreck, trying to hold on to reality. When the police arrived they removed him from the house while I was in the police car explaining to the w.p.c what had happened. I saw the police escort him round the corner, a rush of fear ran through me. The officer I was talking to told me I could have him arrested for rape but by this time I just wanted to crawl into a dark corner.

The police told me there was no evidence of a break in so he walked away with no charge against him. My front door was tampered with and the wood by my back window was split, the police obviously didn't check properly. They also didn't leave my house secure as my back window was left open and he had just walked round the back, over the fence, and by the time I had got my children from my friends house he was standing there in my front room!

This time I didn't feel scared all I wanted to know was why he did that to me. He just kept pleading me not to call the police! It was obvious to me that the police weren't going to help me; in fact they had made things worse! I was in a daze all day, letting him in and out of my house, not wanting him in the house but too scared to do anything about it. That night he slept upstairs and I spent the night on the sofa.

The next day things hit me hard, he was upstairs and I wanted him out. I called the police, I had dialled the local number not 999, I also called my c.p.n and told her what had happened. I was very anxious with him being upstairs so I called the police again and I was assured the police would be attending soon. One hour after my call I still had no response from the police, by this time I was angry and scared that he would wake up soon. I rang them again this time very distressed. Perhaps they didn't want to attend until my nurse was there, as they didn't believe me.

When my nurse arrived she seemed surprised and annoyed with the response from the police. Two hours after my first call the police arrived two male officers and one female, the two male officers went to get him while the female pc talked to me, her whole attitude to me was not very sympathetic and she waited until the other pc brought him down turned him round to face me and then asked me if I wanted him arrested for rape. This was not the way I believe people should be treated; I later found out that the officers who arrived thought I was on drugs!!

I left my house and went to my mother's house, because of all the trauma I was going through my family persuaded me to go to hospital for help. I went there voluntarily and was assessed by a doctor. She told me that I was fine but if I wanted to stay for a break I was welcome to. This time I took my medication to help me sleep and to help me, so I wasn't sectioned. The next morning I was telling a nurse what I felt and what I went through when I turned round and saw him standing there. His father had brought him in for help and he was waiting to see a doctor, I explained to the nurse and made it quite clear to the nurse in charge what that man had done to me. It made no difference as he was admitted to the same ward as me!!!

The next day I discharged myself from the ward, this was against all medical advice but I was mad with them and I was determined never to go back there. And it was the last time!

Sometime after this ordeal I was diagnosed with pre-cancer cells in my cervix, this terrified me I didn't want the whole family to know so I only told my mum. There were so many cells that it was decided to put me under general anesthetic to do the operation. While I was under the anesthetic I began to hyperventilate, I believe this happened because they were doing the operation while I was asleep and I suffered abuse when I was asleep! I was told that I probably wouldn't be able to have any more children as my fertility would be very low. I was very happy with the two little ones I had.

I soon got into another relationship but this time it was with an older man, he didn't take drugs apart from drinking a lot of alcohol; he was a very heavy drinker and with all my problems I was drinking heavily at the weekends. He had brought his three children up on his own and he had never been on holiday abroad, so when my mum gave me some money that dad had left us I was eager to take him on holiday. I spent over two thousand pounds on a lovely holiday in the Greek islands for two weeks we had a wonderful time but when we arrived home he spent the night at his ex wife's house. The relationship ended on rocky grounds.

The council had decided to move me to a different area, it was a bigger house and it was nice to make a fresh start, although I was on my own and drinking heavily. My friends made the effort to come round and see me and one night we decided to go out. We ended up at a big house and these young lads had a party as their parents were away. During this party there was plenty of drink and plenty of drugs going round (I never touched drugs as I had seen what it does to people). I remember dancing away and enjoying myself then everything went black the next thing I remember I was waking up naked in a double bed with a stranger laying next to me. I ran out the door looking for my friend when I found her I was still naked and confused. One of the young lads walked my friend and me home and on the way he told me that they had spiked my drink and then all had sex with me.

The next day I informed the police, I was taken to a house where I had to be examined. This was humiliating, degrading and painful. A week later, two male non-uniformed police came round, they explained to me that in their opinion from what they had investigated I had drunk too much and passed out. I was confused by this comment and asked them if that gave them the right to have sex with me? Then one of them told me to put it down to experience!! This comment threw me completely! I became too scared to go out the house as for all I knew I could pass these men in the street and not know. I had comments shouted out in the street, was approached at the bus stop and called a slag. All this intimidation was too much for me to handle so I dropped all charges and didn't want to know the results of the tests that were done.

This terrible ordeal didn't cause me to go to the hospital as I was determined not ever to go there. After a while I managed to stand tall again. I then met a lovely man. He had heard about what had happened and the things that were said about me, but for the first time in my life I found some one who would listen to me, not judge me or my mental illness, never pressure me into doing anything I didn't want to but above all he was there to listen over and over again until I was sick of telling him. He never thought I was going crazy when I told him about my ex husband abusing me, instead he held me and comforted me. In ten years of illness that was all I needed some one to believe in me and not to judge me.

Two months after meeting this man we were married. He knew about my illness and he knew all about my past. Soon after, to my surprise, I fell pregnant. Life round that area was still hard for me due to the incident that had happened and I was still frightened in case I bumped into any of them so we decided to move away. This was hard for my husband as he had other children in the area and that would mean leaving them, but we often travelled back to see them. My pregnancy had a few problems but doctors took great care of the baby and me throughout. I was induced two weeks early but after seven hours of labour I was only seven centimetres dilated and things weren't progressing. The doctor came in and I was told he was going to do an internal and that it would be quiet rough. He began and I felt as though he was ripping my insides out (I am sure that after many years in and out of psychiatric wards if I were able to tell the doctors what I had been through this wouldn't have happened!) My husband saw the pain in my eyes and told him to stop. After that, two hours later I gave birth to a lovely baby girl, she was in good health and we went home the next day.

A few weeks passed, but then my daughter told my husband and I that her biological father had touched her private parts. After all these years I thought I was strong enough to cope but unfortunately along with other family problems I couldn't and I lost my sanity. Many police cars turned up outside my house, I was terrified by this. My husband knew this and dealt with it by only letting two of them in the house, and by talking with me there was no need for violence or any physical action from the police. I was very ill this time, the hospital where we had moved to couldn't get hold of the medical records from the old hospital and therefore didn't give me e.c.t until a later date. This time I had my husband standing by me and when I went to a tribunal to try and get out early, we won our case. As we walked from the hospital we were told that if I didn't go back there to finish my e.c.t course I WOULD be ill again; not might, WOULD. I turned round and told them that I wouldn't be going back there again and with my husband saying the same thing and standing by me I have not been back there since, that was in 2001; six years ago!

When I got home I was determined to help my daughter and I reported her allegations to the police. The police in this area are from a different police force, they took my daughter to a safe house and did a taped interview. My little girl was very brave and I was so proud of her. As she left the house she turned and said thank you mummy for letting me talk about it; this gave me a great release, a heavy load was lifted of my shoulders. Although the outcome of the investigation was that they couldn't do anything about it as there was not enough criminal evidence, I was happy that some one had listened to her. I have since thought that maybe the police had not done more (as they never asked for the babysitters name) because of my mental illness, nevertheless, I asked police if they could inform the Social Services in the area were we used to live as Mr. X had several children with his new wife. I was assured that they would.

When my youngest daughter was only seven months old I fell pregnant, the pregnancy wasn't planed and it was a shock to us all. I went to the doctors and the first thing he said was "have you considered an abortion?" this upset me deeply as all my children are worth every bit of pain I went through. This time I took advice from psychiatrists, the council moved us to a large house and we settled in well. I had a c.p.n who was quite scatty! She made me laugh and we got on well. There were no problems during the pregnancy, the labour was only two hours, I didn't need any aggressive internals and I was out the hospital within five hours. Also my stepdaughters were with me at home to help me out. Things this time were different, I fed my baby for the first few days then I went on medication I stayed well and with the help of all the people around me, me and my baby boy stayed together.

My problems didn't end there; my daughter was still suffering inside. She was having horrible nightmares but was too scared to tell me as every time she did I wasn't strong enough. Then one day she was strong enough to tell a teacher what she was suffering. She had written a little note to a teacher saying "Why did my dad abuse me? Please someone help me". With this, a social worker came round to our house. She spoke to her on her own and then with me, it was then I discovered how much pain and suffering she was going through, she had started to self harm. With all the anguish she had held inside she found it gave some kind of release. We talked about things and I comforted her. That was the last time she harmed, as the truth was out and I was going to deal with it. Nothing was going to take hold of my emotions and tear my family apart again; I would never lose my sanity or go on another emotional roller coaster. I applied for my notes from Social Services; I needed to know why they didn't help my daughter or me. This was in 2005 now in 2007 I have at last got the answer.....

This is a quote from Social Services:

"when she was ill not only did her behaviour change and she lost insight, but also she became pre-occupied with sexual matters as follows:
- 3rd July 1995 a referral was made by doctor to the mental health team was she was concerned about sexual abuse she had received when she was thirteen.
- 05.07.95 telephone call to social services, she began by stating that her husband was abusing her physically, mentally and sexually.

- 20.07.95 seen on ward 12 following a referral by GP, says she became upset and had to come to hospital because of husband's sexual demands."

For Gods sake, just because I suffered from manic episodes doesn't mean I was lying. I was suffering from manic episodes because of the lack of help in the community. Mental Health was assuming that all my accusations were down to my mental health problems.

Postscript

I HAVE BEEN WELL NOW FOR MANY YEARS AND IV'E BEEN OFF ANY MEDICATION FOR OVER A YEAR NOW. THIS WHOLE EXPERIENCE HAS MADE ME SO EMOTIONALLY STRONG THAT NOTHING WILL EVER KNOCK ME DOWN AGAIN.

THROUGH TEN YEARS OF MENTAL ILLNESS NOT ONCE WAS I OFFERED COUNSELLING. MY COUNSELLER WAS MY HUSBAND, THE ONLY ONE WHO BELIEVED IN ME!!!!!!

COLONIES

By Paul D. Wilson

Published by
Chipmunkapublishing
PO Box 6872
Brentwood
Essex CM13 1ZT
United Kingdom

http://www.chipmunkapublishing.com

Edited by Jurita Bennett

PART ONE

Ants, by nature, are strange. I once thought to myself: does a human being looking at an ant stampede see the same thing as the stampede looking at a human being? The answer, quite simply, is probably not. Ants travel in rivers, in scattered patterns, scavengers of the world of logic. Can we talk to ants? Again, probably not, however their antennae must be attracted to cohesion, to order, much like us humans and our so-called extra sensory perceptions. I conclude that ants know us better than we know ourselves.

The adventure begins in Corsica, an island off the south-east coast of France, 1994 AD:

Madame duPont works hard for a living. She is working hard to defend herself from the traitors who are trying to shut down her hotel.

"Traitors." she mutters under her breath.

A green Ford Ka pulls into the driveway. A man emerges, hands full of boxed paperwork.

"You know nothing," says Madame duPont, again *sotto voce*.

The unnamed man approaches.

"You have been warned." whispers Madame duPont.

What happened next? The sheer and utter wrath of Madame duPont was unleashed on the innocent looking twenty-something, much to his discomfort. Baguettes went flying everywhere.

"Madame," says the man, "we have nothing left to offer you."

"I see." says duPont "You want to boot me out of my hotel, replace it with another hotel. Flippin' fantastic."

Madame duPont is fiercely sarcastic at times. Occasionally she invites friends over for a meal, her husband being deceased. She is fond of bottles of red wine. She is eighty years old, plays an accordion in her spare time and looks wistfully at the azure crystal set into the ring on the fourth finger of her left hand from time to time.

"I apologize" said the man, "sign here please."

Reluctantly, she did, totally aware that underneath that mans shiny, suited exterior lay a heart of absolute zero.

"May I collect my pictures?" asks Madame duPont.

"You have two weeks," replied the man, nonchalantly.

***

Ara, a colonial ant, padded silently down one of the sloping subterranean passageways. This is how she thinks:

"Rumbleabove…rumblebelow…follow follow follow"

Time is experientially different in the ant world. The reason for this, quite simply, is that they don't have clocks.

"Jogarhythm… follow follow"

It had been several egg-cycles since she last saw her mate, Rane, another colonial. In winter, ice had separated them. Ants hate obstacles.

"Rumbleabove", Ara froze, one of the humans was putting rubbish down here again. It stank and reminded her of the time on the beach when she had found a cigarette. Her friend Ini had ventured too close to the hot part and was badly burned.

Smoke began to pour through the passages, so she began to run.

"Rumblerun… fun fun fun"

***

A piece of ant trivia, according to human science: Grind up some ants, put a small amount of ground ants on the end of a cocktail stick and draw on a surface with the "antstick". Mysteriously, living ants will follow the scientists trace. We are unable to explain why this is the case. My theory is that the ants are joking with us. Anyway…

***

"Thoughtrumble… run run run… fun"

Ara turned a corner, and scanned.

"Herenow thoughtrumble"

She waited…

and waited…

and…

"EEEE"

Rane, her mate appeared round the corner and they embraced; feelers together again.

"How long?" asked Rane.

"They are!" replied Ara; she was referring to the long, lost colony in the middle of the town of Calvi. The hotel colony on the hill with the cross had heard only rumours of its existence from the librarians in the archive.

On their way back to the interior, Ara kept saying "icemelt… freenow", over and over again: it was driving Rane to the brink of madness. On the other hand, he knew that it wasn't only their separation that had addled her brain. The poor female wasn't making any sense.

"C'mon," he said, "I'll take you to the archive and we can talk to Squadro."

Ara looked at him zealously. As they vanished down the passageway, Ara kept on chanting: "icemelt… freenow"

Sylvia and Marcus duLac sat eating croissants on the patio of Hotel Ethos. Marcus was on a fact-finding mission for the French Ministry of Agriculture. As an insectologist, Marcus had been sent to the town of Calvi to observe the local ant colonies and come back with a specific portfolio. The FMA was to decide whether a mass culling, or "pest reduction scheme" was plausible.

Sylvia and Marcus' morning conversation ran thus:

"You were tossing and turning all of last night; something wrong, babe?" asked Sylvia.

"These croissants are stale," replied Marcus, "that old lady doesn't have a clue, does she? I mean, doesn't she realise that these insects are literally congregating beneath our feet right now and they really, really like crumbs. Some of them bite, you know? What would happen if…"

"You didn't answer me properly."

"Sorry." apologised Marcus, "I've got tons of measurements to do today."

At once, Madame duPont appeared:

"How are the croissants guys?"

"They are lovely, thanks, Madame." lied Marcus, who promptly received a kick under the table from his girlfriend.

***

Several feet below the surface, Ara the ant was receiving a vast amount of sugar from the moistened cube in the archive.

"Will she be better?" asked Rane.

Squadro the elder allowed a brief smile to cross his mandibles:

"At least she recognizes you; at least she has all six legs and two antennae."

"That's true. What can we do for her?" asked Rane, his concern peaking.

"If you have a compassionate heart, you would know that the best thing for her now is rest." replied Squadro.

"eeeee" sighed Ara, her antennae wilting to the floor.

"Tomorrow," explained Squadro "we will hear her story."

***

It was night-time; Madame duPont sat in a long, silken dressing gown in the master bedroom of the hotel, surveying the occupant information (there were three besides herself):

- A young, business-like couple from Lyon, unashamedly in love.
- An elderly gentleman whose tobacco habit far outranked her own.

Her gaze shifted to the photo of her dead husband. At the age of seventy-five, she felt more and more like his eyes were coming alive again, surveying her as she flitted through the room, occasionally nude. What were the young couple downstairs doing? She heard giggling and talk of croissants. It gave her pleasure to hear them carry on. Moonbeams flickered through the Venetian blinds and she managed at last to rest, safe in the knowledge that the physical (or spiritual?) distance between her and her beloved was growing smaller each day that she breathed the air of planet Earth.

"Eyes open, Ara, tell us your story" said Squadro.

She began:

"Much calmer now must talk must talk there were six… six… six of us. It was the expedition to the pool, the paddling pool… by the pool were sweet-things. Me be lonely female of six. Five, four, three, two and one were huntergathering sweet-things by the paddling pool. Me resist the sweet-things, went for nest material instead. THEN BOOT COME DOWN SQUASH FIVE EEEEE!... EEEEE."

"More sugar, Rane" said Squadro, listening intently.

Ara began again:

"Nestmaterial no good, it was plastic from straw for human use. THEN BOOT COME DOWN SQUASH FOUR EEEEE!... EEEEE!... there was, there was entrapment now for three of us. We three go into shrubs to hide from boot. Then giant rubber-thing get thrown into pool. Human dive in. Human get out, get dressed. Other two make their way slowly to sweet-thing again. Then I get lost inside drainpipe; find myself next to many many dead ants. Was horrible, horrible. I hear screams of three and two."

"And then the storm came, right Ara?" asked Rane.

"Ssssh!" instructed the elder, "let her finish."

"Stormdrain, stormdrain, many dead ants around me, no life, only death, there were so many…"

"That's enough for now, Ara" said Squadro, and sent her instantly into dormancy with an antennae bolt.

Silence filled the archive.

"Why, Squadro, why?" asked Rane, looking at his beautiful mates shell, which was now devoid of movement.

"You know exactly why." replied Squadro, and set about spinning a crystallinette to cocoon her in.

Rane and Squadro hummed together in agreement (ants do <u>not</u> cry as a rule). Ara's body was carried by two other colonials over to the far corner of the archive and placed solemnly on the wall. The crystallinette glowed magical colours whilst it aided the healing process. Squadro sang a testament to the five other members of the scouting party whilst Rane projected his thoughts over the horizon, knowing that soon he and Ara would be reunited as mates.

"Look you, that was terrible" said Sylvia.

"I've got a lot on my mind at the moment" replied Marcus.

"What kind of excuse is that?"

"Okay, I've got ants in my pants, geddit?"

"So tell me what you have to do" said Sylvia, calming a little.

"Well… tomorrow morning I've got to collect samples" explained Marcus, walking naked over the carpet to the small, brown briefcase he had brought with him. He unlocked it gently and lifted the lid, showing Sylvia the collection jar and various company pesticides he was to use on the ants.

"Tomorrow?" queried Sylvia, "well in that case you had better come back to bed."

The lights went off and the young lovers entwined once again in the milky shadows of a Corsican night.

***

Underground, mysterious things were starting to occur:

Rane had been instructed to go back to his nest by Squadro, who was busy singing to Ara's crystallinette. A few colonials had decided to get drunk behind the hotel bar on a few drops of grappa and had been sent to the queen room for reprobation. Ara's body was beginning to glow in the traditional fashion, whilst Rane told everyone in his nest to hold a nightlong vigil, knowing full-well that they didn't really care and would be asleep within minutes.

Throughout all this, Squadro continued to sing quietly, his voice echoing through the tunnels.

***

Rane awoke the next morning to find the other colonials still asleep. He decided to return to the archive on his own whilst Squadro snoozed. (Even elders need their rest, if not more so than younger ants.)

He approached Ara's resting place and decided to try the revival process for himself.

Okay here goes, he thought:

Rane's antennae began to quiver, and he felt earth energy filling his body. *One, Two, Three...*

Two bolts of blue lightning shot from him and landed directly in Ara's heart centre. The crystallinette glowed green. He waited for a minute while the green colour faded, knowing that he wasn't really supposed to be doing this.

At that precise moment, Squadro entered the archive. He looked furious...

"What in the name of the queen are you doing?" he shouted angrily.

"It's too late," replied Rane, "look!"

The crystallinette was melting. Bits and pieces of it fell all over the floor in shards. The very last thing to happen was incredible: Ara became unstuck from the wall and landed directly on all six legs, her eyes now glowing an electric blue. She was fine!

Squadro looked on, completely and utterly surprised. Silence filled the archive for a few moments until Rane spoke up at last:

"I think we three had better go and see the queen."

The queen room was vast. An array of drones protected the majestic creature herself from attacks by unfaithfuls. Sine, Square and Sawtooth, the unlucky trio who had been caught drinking grappa, were marched, or rather pulled into the queens abode.

Sawtooth, the most indignant of the three, also the one who had drunk the most was the first to dissent.

"I object to this treatment." he guffawed drunkenly.

"Stand aside drones." said the queen.

At once, the drones parted, something akin to Moses parting the Red Sea.

"Speak up then." gestured the queen.

"We are *extremely* bored here, your majesty." said Sawtooth.

The queen murmured inwardly. The thousands of unborn inside her were communicating to her brain what to say. After a pause:

"Never forget who gave birth to you; never forget that I could have you annihilated in a matter of moments." she said with a voice that sounded more like a group creature than a single entity.

Consequently, Sine, Square and Sawtooth sobered up drastically. Their original plan involved escape, three female younglings and an attempt to reach the castle colony in the middle of Calvi. Unfortunately, they hadn't really thought it through. Long ago, there had been a schism between the castle colony and the hotel colony; the distance between the two was great and there were an enormous variety of ways in which ants could get killed trying to reach their brethren. Ants do not like motor vehicles or roads.

"I have often announced my dislike for treacherous traitors such as you three." said the queen.

Sawtooth began again: "With respect, your majesty, the barriers that you have set up in order to stop us reaching our brothers are non-existent, in my opinion. With time and a little…"

"**Do not question us again.**" barked the queen, her shiny black hulk quivering now. She was preparing to lay eggs and some of the drones had a murderous glint in their eyes.

Square, the most sensible of the three, decided to pipe up:

"Sawtooth, if you don't stop this, we are going to get ourselves killed!" he whispered to his friend.

Sawtooth carried on without taking heed:

"When will the truth be revealed about the castle colony, when will we be reunited?"

Five drones approached Sawtooth and grabbed him suddenly, their poisonous mandibles bit into him viciously and he let out a terrible scream.

"Sine, Square, run now and gather others, tell them what we know, this place is **against**!" he said before he was taken off to be fed to the newborn.

Sine and Square bolted for the nearest exit and managed to escape a venomous demise, the dying screams of their companion following them down the tunnels.

***

Splash! Marcus dived into the hotel swimming pool. It was a rubbish attempt. His swimming shorts were far too big and he ended up naked underwater. Sylvia giggled gaily as she watched her boyfriend try and rectify his shame.

"You know we should all be naked really." she laughed.

"When we're swimming? There'd be a lot of underwater births!" said Marcus.

"Oh, you." she said and giggled some more.

"Christ!" shouted Marcus suddenly.

"What is it my love?" asked Sylvia.

"Just got stung by a wasp. Do you think I should ask the FMA about the wasp population here as well?" Marcus commented dryly.

"I think you should just stick to what you're supposed to do." said Sylvia and noticed that Marcus was nodding his head secretively towards the patio. Sylvia turned her head and saw an old man with his back turned to them, smoking a traditional French pipe. Madame DuPont appeared with some honey for his bread.

"How come the wasps aren't after him?" asked Marcus quietly.

"Maybe he's in a pact with them. He could be a giant wasp man who has been sent here to thwart your plans," said Sylvia, and added: "We should go and speak to him. Get dry."

The old man barely moved his eyes when the couple came and sat at the adjacent table to him.

"*Bon jour.*" said Marcus in a polite manner.

The old man said nothing and moved only to light his pipe once more and puff heartily on it.

"Leave him alone." whispered Sylvia in Marcus' ear, "If he doesn't want to speak to us then we should leave him alone."

"*Bon jour, monsieur?*" said Marcus, in a slightly more surly tone.

It had no effect: the old man just sat there.

As the couple were about to walk into the bar, the old man spoke:

"Great danger, I warn you." he said mysteriously.

"What do you mean?" asked Marcus.

"Nature does not like to be disturbed, especially when it is no threat to you or anyone else." said the old man, and went silently back to smoking his pipe.

"C'mon Marcus, he's clearly deranged or something. Let's go shopping now." said Sylvia.

"Oh, babes, you can go if you like, I have measurements to make this morning." said Marcus, sensing Sylvia's haste to leave the hotel.

"Fine." she said and walked towards the stairwell.

Marcus looked back, and to his amazement the old man was nowhere to be seen. Marcus did the only thing possible in this kind of situation; he went to the bar and ordered a cool beer.

Rane and Ara were alone once again. On their way to see the queen, Squadro had decided that he had important business to attend to with another elder.

"I didn't think you were going to make it." said Rane tenderly.

"I am here." said Ara, "While I was asleep I heard you and Squadro singing to me in my dreams."

"The crystallinettes are here to help, but they can only heal physical ailments. If there was some way of taking away the hurt that I felt when we were apart then I would be there in a moment." said Rane.

"There is..." said Ara, and let her antennae entwine with Rane's. Pink rings formed around their double-body whilst they shared a brief connection.

"…no such thing as distance." said Rane, finishing Ara's words.

"What now?" asked Ara.

"I must leave you briefly, to go and find Squadro and the tribune. Only the elders can tell us what's going on right now. I'm sure I heard a colonial die a short time ago. No doubt the drones would have had something to do with it." said Rane bitterly.

"Go then. I will meet you further on…"

Marcus, now dressed in his work outfit, a cream shirt, brown tie and grey trousers, set to work measuring the patio.

"Five feet by three feet," he stated to himself, "this would be an ideal place to start."

He spotted a group of ants underneath the nearest table and gave them a vigorous squirt of company pesticide. At first, they acted normally, picking up crumbs and dragging them back to wherever. Then, one by one, they began to lean onto their sides, three legs on the ground and three in the air, their antennae flailing wildly. Whatever this stuff was it seemed to be doing the trick! After a few minutes all of their movement had ceased. The ants seemed to be… melting, giving off a pungent odour. After a few more minutes, the ants were nothing but stains on stone. Marcus noted this in his notebook and went off to make some more measurements.

***

Madame DuPont was busy in the kitchen, making bread from a machine. She was so absorbed in her task that she failed to notice the elderly gentleman behind her. She turned around and received a tremendous shock.

"Sacre bleu!" she exclaimed.

The old man looked bemused:

"I can see you are passionate with your hands," he said.

"Please refrain from smoking your pipe in the kitchen." she replied.

"Are you lonely here?" he asked.

Madame duPont looked a little deeper into his hazel eyes. Secretly, she was reminded of her husband.

"Not at all." she lied.

"But surely, you need help? Geddit? *Knead* help?" he joked.

"Monsieur Auberge, I find your advances insulting, now would you please return to the bar if you wish to smoke." she said waspishly.

The old man left the kitchen, taking a little piece of her heart with him.

***

"Look, Rane, you can't just stroll in here as if you own the place." said Squadro.

The council room had a pleasant atmosphere, like that of an old library. The elders were scattered around, humming and writing on crusts. In the middle sat Corto, the wisest elder of them all.

"I hope you've got a decent explanation for being here." prompted Squadro.

Rane paused for thought, and then said:

"On my way here, I bumped into two old friends of mine: Sine and Square. They told me that Sawtooth, a jumped-up colonial from the barracks, had just been killed in the line of duty, so to speak."

"No need to explain, Rane," started Corto in a husky voice, "we already know that the young drones are becoming more and more violent. The reason for this is simple, our colony is overcrowded. The queen is pregnant, more so than ever, and we need to branch out and find new space to live."

"Then why are we still here?" asked Rane.

Corto smiled with a thousand peaceful smiles:

"Because, you little upstart, the journey from here to the other colony is dangerous, more dangerous than you might realise. We need to plan carefully. Sawtooth was killed for a reason; to demonstrate that haste is not always the quickest solution. Do you understand?"

Rane nodded in sympathy.

"Now you must fetch your mate, Ara. We are to send you both ahead as emissaries for the colony. The road will be long and the human threat will be very real, but we have seen ahead that you can make it with the correct company. Do you understand?"

"Company?"

"Squadro will travel with you." explained the wisest of the elders.

Squadro looked up and ceased humming. He hadn't seen this coming. He thought about speaking his mind, but inwardly he knew that his own powers were limited and Corto had a very good point: Ara and Rane would need his help getting to the castle.

Corto added:

"Now go and find the female, and be careful."

Squadro and Rane looked at each other, knowing that the real journey had only just begun.

Squadro and Rane spent the next morning trying to convince Ara that the three of them were not going to get killed on the way to the castle.

"We will never make it," she commented pessimistically.

"That's probably true," said Squadro, trying to outwit her negativity.

"I think the sooner we get going the better, Ara, now are you with us or not?" challenged Rane.

"Okay, let's go for it." said Ara and the trio duly left the nest, once and for all.

Firstly, they came across a flattened bird on the road.

"This doesn't bode well," said Ara.

The carcass was tasty and provided them with much nourishment. After their meal, Rane scouted around to check for vibrations. Many an ant had been squashed by motor vehicles at this very spot.

"Do you think we'll meet anyone else?" asked Rane of Squadro.

"Possibly, maybe." he replied.

***

Inside the queen room, her majesty was about to give birth to thousands of baby ants. The drones sang an anthem, completely unaware that Marcus, above on the patio, was pouring liquid pesticide onto the nest. As it seeped into the interior, the colony turned into a panic zone. Males, females and children ran hither and thither, trying to escape the deadly tides that were now washing through the tunnels. Their attempts to escape were futile;

soon the stench of death was everywhere. The last to die were the drones and the queen herself, who managed somehow to climb out of the nest and gaze defiantly at Marcus' shoes as his spray can wiped them forever from existence.

PART TWO

The colonel marched quickly into the entrapment chamber, a space between the inner and outer walls of Calvi citadel. His name was Boros, the first of a giant mutant breed that fed solely off ice creams. A frightened youngster in the town centre once saw Boros snap the remaining wooden stick of an ice cream in half, and promptly complained to his parents.

"It seems we may have trouble," announced Boros to three guards. The guards clickety-clacked their way to the main gate and prepared their killing jaws for fighting.

***

Ara and Rane stood quietly next to each other on the road to Calvi citadel. Squadro, the elder, maintained that the berries they were eating were poisonous. So as not to disturb his companions, he sat for a few minutes silently meditating on the friends that they had lost.

"These taste alright," said Ara to Rane.

"I bet our elder is sat in meditation, you know communicating with the crystallinettes."

"You males and those damn sugarthings." suggested Ara, hoping that Rane would take more notice of her.

At this point, a car drove not more than a few centimetres from their heads, nearly squishing them to bits.

"It just goes to show how fragile life can be," suggested Rane, hoping that Ara might take more notice of cars.

"Right-e-o, let's get going again!" shouted Squadro, "I believe there may be an edible shrub just around the corner."

***

The three guards from the citadel took less than half a day to travel the distance to the spot where Ara, Rane and Squadro were hiding. It was night-time and the three good ants were baffled by sounds coming from the edible shrub.

"Eeek!" screamed Ara in sympathy to the ensuing attack.

Mandibles flew and jaws locked in a whirlwind of violence. It took several minutes for the victors to become apparent.

"Phew!" said Ara.

"Crikey." said Rane

"Rogues!" shouted a fazed elder at the three husks that lay before them, the moon casting ironic shadows from their bulky frames.

As the trio left the fighting ground for the hopefully the last time, Rane took a backward glance at the unconscious guards and smirked in triumph.

Monsieur Jel, the official, pulled up in his purple Volkswagen to Hotel Ethos. Today was a day for breaking bad news.

"Madame duPont," he stated calmly, "I'm afraid…"

"It's alright, I know, you're going to close me down," she replied.

"I'm afraid so."

Later, the Madame took one last, long look out to sea from her bedroom window and remembered that she still had the elderly gentleman for company.

Pour chaque anniversaire,

C'est une bombe,

Une lumiere,

Et surprise.

"This must be it!" said Rane excitedly.

"It is," replied Squadro in his wisdom, "I have exact knowledge of this place. You never got to see the maps Rane, I'm sorry."

"But I did!" squeaked Ara, "I snuck into library once and read the squiggles. We have to go in through there."

Rane and Squadro followed Ara's pointed antennae to a small gap under some stone steps. There were children everywhere and Squadro had to protect them from being squashed by human feet with ant magic.

The citadel was a vast, labyrinthine maze of stone and shrouds of gardens, mostly decayed in the present day, although tourists might imagine the once regal luminescence of days gone by.

"Okay Ara, where now?" asked Squadro once they were inside.

"Know not I," she replied.

Rane suggested that they should find food in the kitchens, but at that precise moment, a colonel appeared.

"I hope you find our nest to your satisfaction," he stated as six or so guards marched straight in and grabbed the trio, "Please state your name and place of origin."

Squadro chimed in: "We're from Hotel Ethos, a colony north of here, we only seek refuge."

"Let them go," dictated the superior, "And give them what they need."

The six guards; one of whom had only four legs, released their grip on the newcomers and instructed them not to try and escape back through the way they had come in. Already the three suspected trouble.

***

Inside their room, the trio pondered their fate inside the vast citadel. They heard ants scurrying to and fro, even the smaller ones that were invisible to humans.

"Let us now contemplate the uncertain future," said Squadro and as he looked up, realised that the other two were locked in an embrace.

"We three," he continued, "Should remain calm in the midst of the elegant grand design…" He was a short note away from being the mainstay elder that he once used to be. Ara and Rane continued to cuddle whilst Squadro tip-toed out into the courtyard.

"Look around brother," announced an unfamiliar voice, "You will see that here ants and shoes are all that we have."

A large ant, smaller than Boros but bigger than Squadro had a look of wisdom about him:

"May I call myself Geo, yes I suppose I can…" his voice trailed off at the end.

"Squadro," bowed Squadro.

"Geo. I am the least intelligent of the ants here, which may make me the wisest," his voice continued to trail off at the end, "although I should warn you that this courtyard is haunted, by myself."

The ant called Geo disappeared, leaving Squadro wondering where he had gone. It took him a few moments for him to click; Geo had flown into the air with a pair of wings!

"Geo, why are you flying ants so willing to demonstrate your powers?" laughed Squadro, watching Geo hover back and forth in the air.

"Follow me on foot if you like…" shouted Geo, and vanished across the courtyard. Squadro followed him as fast as he could.

***

Ara and Rane awoke later to find Squadro standing over them.

"Now we are locked in," announced Squadro.

"Oh, what happened?" asked Ara and Rane together.

"I was fussy about the food here. I met a flying ant called Geo who took me to their library and I told him that the records were mouldy. He looked a bit annoyed. Then, I told him that I could do with a bite to eat. At that point I went with him to the eating hall and suddenly another ant knocked into me and sugar went all over the place. I broke several of the citadel rules by offering to clean up and then I got brought back here."

"On the way I noticed that everyone was staring at me, it was most peculiar," finished Geo.

"So what do we do?" asked Rane.

"We escape!" cried out Ara, pointing at the ceiling. The smaller ants, anants, were disappearing through a crack in the roof, where a large sugar cube seemed to be sticking out.

"You mean we eat our way out?" asked Rane.

"You first!" replied Ara.

Ara, Rane and Squadro found themselves in an upper room, at first surprised by the cool, fresh air blowing in through a cross-shaped window. The window looked out onto the esplanade where human tourists mingled by the hundreds, eating ice creams and feasting on seafood.

"If I've offended the locals then we should probably try and escape," suggested Squadro.

'PRIVATE RECORDS' read a sign on the wall, written in sugar.

Ara hunched herself up, presumably communicating, and then suddenly let out one her abominable cries.

"Ara, sssh, you'll get us caught," said Rane.

"Don't worry, she's found something. What is it Ara?" said Squadro.

"The anants here are deadly," whispered Ara, quietly.

As they looked around, they heard scuttling. Squadro looked up and saw hundreds of anants swarming on the ceiling, slowly creeping down the four walls. They had to act quickly, so they climbed out the window and used the sticky pads on their feet to keep a grip on the vertical stone. Rane nearly lost his back legs escaping from the little fire-breathers.

"Now what?" asked Ara.

"We climb down and get away from this place," suggested Rane, only to find Squadro nearly halfway to the bottom. The fire-ants were pouring out the window in the thousands now and very nearly managed to get Ara, Rane grabbed her with his jaws and jumped, falling all the way down to a restaurant below. They fell directly into some human's soup. Fortunately the man was having a conversation at the time, and they managed to climb over the edge, drenched in tomatoes.

"Pssst, down here," shouted Squadro, waggling his antennae wildly and narrowly avoided a human toddler's attempts to squash him with a piece of baguette.

***

Ara, Rane and Squadro, having avoided certain death, formed cocoons at the restaurant. There were a few ants here and there; plain local ants picking up crumbs. About eight in the morning, an enormous series of bangs resounded throughout the town; the humans were holding a festival with cannons. Ara stirred from her coon and ventured slowly on her own out into the quiet of the open-air restaurant. She nibbled on breadcrumbs here and there, pausing occasionally to look at the view. Something stirred behind her. An enormous fire-ant with a red body was dragging a piece of baguette somewhere else.

"Who are you?" exclaimed Ara.

"My name's March. I know who you are," said the fire-ant, towering over her.

At this moment, Squadro and Rane appeared, readying for battle.

"I fear you will be eaten if you come any closer," said March.

"Who are you, exactly?" asked Squadro.

The enormous red ant pointed a leg at Ara; "That's my daughter..."

"What?" begged Rane.

"I promise you, that's my daughter," said March, "She's half fire-ant and extremely clairvoyant."

Ara took a few seconds to assess March and then let out an enormous shriek:

"EEEE!" she cried.

Squadro felt like nearly attacking the fire-ant, although he was nearly twice the size of him. Eventually, he bowed in an act of succumbing.

"Kind ant, please explain how Ara came to be made," said Squadro.

"Her mother was a titch; very, very small yet kind," explained March, "and particularly sensitive. She used to communicate with the sea life down at the water's edge. One day, we mated and Ara was born the next year. From a young age she was acutely aware."

"Cute as well," said Rane.

Ara looked ready to explode:

"No no no, we parted at young age. Where did you go?" asked Ara.

"I've been at the restaurant ever since, dragging crumbs around for the local hive. You wouldn't remember the day I took you to the hotel," said March, hastening on to another table with the bread in tow; "Would you three like to meet the queen?"

Ara, Rane and Squadro bowed meekly and followed March.

The inside of the nest was red, underneath the main part of the restaurant, shrouded by a canopy. Ants were scattered here and there and the smell of freshly baked bread pervaded the nest.

"This is where we live," explained March, "We've been here forever. One day, after the citadel was built, we branched away."

"That's my father," explained Ara to Squadro and Rane, who were disbelieving at first but slowly came round to that fact.

March was about the same size as Geo, the flying ant and completely red. He told them that he very rarely used his venomous jaws to kill, although he would if any ant from the citadel should try and break into the nest. The two factions had been in a feud ever since the day he had told them of.

A female ant came over to them carrying a piece of bread for each of the four (March's was twice the size of the others).

"Good afternoon, travellers. Hi March. My name is Fract and I presume you would like to see the queen. She lives down the hall. Please follow," explained the newcomer.

Squadro made his way first into the queen's chamber. A vast ant lay sprawled across the marble floor like a figurine.

"Speak," said the queen.

Taking a few moments to communicate, Squadro began:

"Ma'am we are, or rather were, from a northern colony at Hotel Ethos, which became unstable and was sadly destroyed. The queen there was bitter and didn't rule properly. It came to us that the only thing to do was escape. We traversed the winding roads down to the main town and found ourselves at the citadel, where we were treated as prisoners. Having escaped that place, we wound up here as your respectful guests, ma'am."

"I see," said the queen, "Give him what he needs, and send in the other two."

Rane and Ara stumbled in and prostrated themselves before the majestic black ant.

"I see that you two are in love," said the queen at once, "What do you have to say?"

"We are but strangers here," said Rane quietly.

"Majesty feel alright; no more killings," said Ara.

"What do we call you?" asked Rane, impatient.

"Call me Majesty," replied the queen, "Because that's what I am."

***

Squadro was resting in his room when a sugar letter arrived through the door, carried by a soldier. The elder hurriedly ate it and communicated it back through the crystallinette sitting in the corner of his room.

"The wasps are coming," Squadro said out loud to no one in particular apart from himself, "Please help us if you can. Signed, Majesty."

Squadro sat in silence for a few minutes, digesting the news. Suddenly, Ara and Rane appeared through the door. Squadro informed them of what he had just heard.

"We may be in trouble. Do you remember the bees?" asked Squadro.

"Stingsting, we may fightfight," said Ara in reply.

"Whatever happens," chimed in Rane, "We'll be at your side Squadro. We came to inform you that there is a feast in the main hall."

Back in the main hall the ants, as promised, were holding a communal meal for the entire colony. Crumbs were being brought from the restaurant with haste and a massive pile of pizza dough was being built in the centre of the room. Ants came in sixes to get their portion and then sat around in the same groups. Majesty was sat at the front on her own.

Ara, Squadro and Rane sat with March and two other ants who introduced themselves as Foot and Frolic.

"I hear that your colony suffered an attack from the wasps last month. Our colony was much the same," announced Squadro to the foreign three.

"That's right," piped up Foot and Frolic who appeared to be twins and spoke as one, "We had major damage to our food supply as the little devils tried to take away all of our sugar supplies."

"Food in our colony was always being ravaged," said Rane.

"They steeeeal!" shrilled Ara.

As the six of them munched away, Squadro started becoming bothered. He noticed a pain in his antennae and looked the way of Majesty. She was calling him.

"We have much to discuss in preparation for a flying bombardment," she said to him privately, later, "I recommend that you get as much rest as you can. Gather your two companions and at sunrise go out to the sea to make your last dying wishes. I fear we may not withstand this time…"

It was a bitter message, but as Squadro pondered the queen's words, he became aware once again of his old age and made ready to sleep.

Ara and Rane awoke the next day to find Squadro standing next to them.

"It is time for us to depart," said Squadro.

Slowly the trio made their way through the restaurant and down to the harbour's edge. They looked out at a blissful Corsican sunrise.

"Beauty in sunshine," gasped Ara.

Several minutes passed as Rane and Squadro said their final male prayers together. Suddenly, the three heard cries coming from the restaurant. Ants were beginning to flock from the nest and out to the restaurant floor.

"The wasps are attacking," shouted one ant, as Ara, Rane and Squadro took up their fighting positions.

First, it started as a buzzing, and then slowly the gargantuan nemeses appeared, swaying to and fro in the air, trying to maintain their balance against the Earth. They were hunting for sugar, although any ant that might get in their way would make a tasty meal. Their stings were lethal to our friends.

A wasp made for the ant that had alerted all the others. The ant screamed as a poisoned barb made its way into his body and the foe dragged him into the air, its yellow and black body pulsating with evil, wings flapping fast.

"Noooo!" shouted the ant's mate; she followed soon after at the hands of another wasp.

Soon the air was full of noise. The enemy was everywhere. Panic and hostility was coming from the antennae of all the insects, even the flies, and ants were getting killed everywhere by the feet of the restaurant's morning staff. It was doubtful whether the wasps were sometimes the more dangerous creature.

"Protect the nest entrance!" shouted an ant to six others, and the group huddled blocking the entrance in a pattern. Squadro immediately knew why Majesty had sent them outside; it appeared that the entrance to the nest was not going to hold, and soon the air was filled with a different kind of buzzing, a more familiar one. Squadro looked upward.

"Geo!" he exclaimed.

The flying ants from the citadel were here, and it soon became apparent why: they were here to rescue the ants from the restaurant. Gradually, the flying brigade began picking the land-dwellers into the air and taking them back to their own home, the citadel.

Ara, Rane and Squadro stood in a triangular pattern and began shrieking to attract attention.

"Down there!" shouted Geo, and him and another flyer swooped down to gather the trio. Between Squadro and Rane was Ara; being carried in-between the other two was like being stretched on a rack, and she was squealing non-stop.

"Eeeee!" she cried.

Slowly the wasps were bombarding the entrance to Majesty's nest, and it was giving away. First one ant, then two then three were being picked off by the deadly venom of the wasps. The last four ants simply scattered and then were killed later. The wasps stormed the nest and the noise of the carnage was evident as there were screams from deep inside the nest, as Majesty and her last survivors were dispatched.

Flying through the air, with the lost balloons of tourists below, was a relief, but not fun seeing as Majesty and the colony had apparently been slaughtered. Ara, Squadro and Rane were set down on a landing pad at the top of the citadel, a small circular shape of stone, set into the roof.

"What happened?" inquired Geo, the other flying ants setting down the rescued into the circle.

"Wasp attack," gasped Ara after her ordeal, "many gone now."

For a while, Rane and Squadro said nothing, simply glad to be alive, although miserable.

"It looks like the restaurant colony just wasn't meant to be. I remember when it got started," finished Geo, flying back down to the restaurant floor, "Get inside to avoid the wasps."

It was true; the wasps were already making their way towards the citadel roof. Geo had to loop and dive to avoid collisions with the deadly aggressors. Squadro, Ara and Rane hurried inside as promised. Once inside, they met March.

Ara struggled to shriek as normal, but instead gave her father an enormous embrace.

"It's alright little one, we're safe now. I fear you may have much to do in the future," said March

It was many months before any of the ants now living in the citadel dared to go back outside. Very few ventured out every now and then to find food. At the height of summer, the wasps reigned supreme. The ants remained in long trails outside to make themselves appear larger, and the colony at the citadel remained united.

Boros, the giant colonel ant addressed everyone in the citadel in the main hall:

"We may go through strife, we may have a hive mind that can be chipped away at by enemies, but they will never undo us. Remember our ant-words: *'Wisdom comes in numbers.'*"

MY FIGHT AGAINST A LIFE OF DEPRESSION

By G. A. Williams

Published by
Chipmunkapublishing
PO Box 6872
Brentwood
Essex CM13 1ZT
United Kingdom

http://www.chipmunkapublishing.com

Edited by Kimberley Bishop

This is my life story.
My mum and brother gave me the inspiration to write it.
They both died in 2001 within a fortnight of one another.

Chapter One – My Childhood

I was born in Coventry in a place called Meriden at the end of the last war in 1944. Coventry was badly bombed with doodlebugs. They bombed factories, hospitals, houses, etc. Coventry was bombed to the ground. It took years before they built it up again. I remember my mum hiding under the table with a teapot in her hand. The bombs came and cracked the teapot and all the tea ran out.

My mother was born in Austria and came over in 1937. My father was a Scotsman. He was a reserve in the Royal Air Force. He was a flight engineer. My mum met my brother's father, which was her first husband, and had my brother. He was born in 1938. He was evacuated to Ampleforth in Yorkshire. Mum met my dad in 1942 and had me in 1944. I went to a nursery at two and then went to an infant school. In the nursery I used to put toys up my knickers-leg, but my mum brought them back the next day. I was a trying and difficult child to bring up. I once put a cat in a tub. I thought it could swim. I ate coal and put a pearl up my nose and swallowed a cufflink. I dragged a dog on my skipping rope and was mad on bikes. I peddled up the middle of the road.

I did not listen to what I was told. I went to a few schools and at the age of eight I went to a boarding school called St Catherine's. It was built for King Henry VIII for one of his mistresses. It was a castle right on top of a hill with lovely grounds and a big driveway with a big green and huge Yew tree. The headmaster was a professor of psychology and he ran it with his wife. I was there six years. I was very unhappy for a while, homesick until I got used to it. But the last few years I was unhappy and mum took me out and I went to a secondary modern school. I was there for two years before I went to work.

Chapter Two – My Teenage Life

I worked at a greyhound track at fifteen. For three years I was a kennel maid, my best job ever and I really enjoyed and loved it. It used to break my heart when the dogs got put down through accident, racing or got too old and finished racing.

I loved my teenage years as I could go out and do my own thing. Dancing was the love of my life and roller skating and swimming and cinema and I could really escape in the pictures and speedway. I loved motorbikes. If I did not have a friend to go with I would go on my own. I was, in a way, a lone wolf. I used to enjoy myself though I had a lot of jobs – all sorts, usherette, car cleaner and mirror packer. I used to make crisps. It was a horrible job. People could smell you when you got on the bus, like a fish and chip shop.

At 15 I had an older boyfriend who wanted to marry me. He was 17, but my dad said he was too old. My brother said he was like a cracked-up speedway rider. I had a lot of one night stands but sometimes they did not turn up and I would wait in rain or snow for an hour. Other girls would only wait 10 minutes – how silly I was. I met my first husband at 17. We went out for two years, got engaged and got married on December 14th before Christmas 1963. I had what you would call a shotgun wedding. It was the done thing in those days. I did not really love him as it was all too quick. That was the end of my single years.

Chapter Three – My First Marriage and Divorce

I really tried and wanted my marriage to work though I did not really love him. He had some not nice habits and was slovenly. Things lay about and got rusty. He was not tidy. I was the opposite, clean and tidy and a bit house proud, but not to make him miserable. He was a bit on the lazy side. I was all for doing-up the house nice, not a palace, just a nice little home.

When I had my first little baby it was a boy. I was happy when I was on my own with him. I loved him very much. I took him out. In those days you could leave your baby out in the garden to get plenty of fresh air. He was so good he slept for hours. He was only 16 months when I was expecting again and had a little girl. She was heavier than the boy. I had a bad birth and nearly died, haemorrhaged. I was so weak and poorly when I took her out in the pram - the pram was holding me up. After six weeks I had a nervous breakdown.

I was married to my first husband for six years then we broke up. I was very distraught and did a silly thing. I admitted to doing something I did not do but it looked bad for me. I went to London to work for five years. I got divorced. After six months my father died and it broke my heart.

Chapter Four – My Breakdown

I was in hospital for six weeks and was very ill. I was in a ward with senile women who touched my bed and stared at me. I was only 21, so young. They used to lash out but I never got hit. They had treatments called ECT. They all came out of a room looking white as sheets. I said to the nurse what has happened to them? That's when she told me about ECT. I was taken to another ward and little did I know I was to have that treatment. I was always the first on the bed. They used to have all the beds together in the wards and covered with white sheets. I shall never forget the experience. It was shocks to the brain. It was horrible. After, you just had to lay and keep still, have a sleep, then get up for a cup of tea. They gave you an injection for drying up your saliva before treatment.

I was in and out a few times and always had ECT. Once, they could not get anything out of me so they gave me pentathol (truth drug). Before a breakdown the first one is breaking down, crying until you vomit and shaking so that you can't hold anything in your hands. I could not even dress my children or hold a cup of tea.

Chapter Five

I went to London after my divorce. For five years I worked in a NAFFI canteen. My manageress always watched me. I thought she was a tyrant as she always went on at me. I kept breaking down and crying for the children. She said if you keep on you will end up in a mental home and you will be no good to yourself or to your children. The girls who worked in Imperial Court as waitresses were good to me. They took me out every weekend. After seven months in London I met a man who I had an affair with for three years. He was married but no children otherwise I would not have gone with him. His wife went her way and he went his. It was great. He took me about to all the places I would have never seen – the nice places and the not so nice – to let me see the other side of London. We went dancing, football trips, out every Sunday clubbing (jazz clubs) as he was fond of jazz, and holidays abroad to Spain, Majorca, Belgium, Holland plus all the places in England. After three years I finished with him as I could not see that he was ever going to leave his maisonette, he was too selfish for that.

I went with a chef in the NAFFI. He was no good so I just went my own way after that. The girls left London, the hostel closed and I ended in a bed-sit. Not a nice room, brown paintwork and small. I stayed there for three years and eventually came to live in Margate where my mum and step-father had a guest house.

Chapter Six - My years in Margate and Marriage Two

After London I came to live in Margate and got a job as a chamber maid. I had a lot of jobs in Margate which were only for a short time. I had a bad depression when my first husband took the children to live in Australia. I was really sick and took an overdose of tablets. I was so sick I did not want to come out of the bed and I hid like a mouse in a hole. I did not want daylight to come. I went into hospital for treatment. The manageress brought me home from work. I went in hospital a couple of times. I came out and met my second husband. I was only going out with him for ten months. We got married in a registry office. We had a lot of up and downs, a love and hate relationship.

One day I had a letter from my first husband to say my daughter was coming to live with me if that was alright. I jumped at the chance to give her a chance to get to know me. It did not work out as I thought. She smoked and took money out of my husband's jacket. She went on a bike without a helmet so I had to go to court and pay a fine. She played me up. She did not want to have new shoes for school so she cut them, also her boots.

My mum noticed that she was lopsided a bit on her right shoulder. From x-rays we found out she had a curvature of the spine and an S-bend.

I took her to clinics and she had to have a hospital bed. She had weights down by her feet and had to be strapped up like a mummy every night and she had to wear a brace from the neck down to her hips and exercise at least five times a day. She had terrible pains in her spine so she skipped school. In the end I asked them if she could have the operation as the spine was going over more and she was in more and more pain. I wanted it to be me. In the end she had the operation or she would have been a cripple and would have gone lopsided. She had a steel rod in her spine down her back. She was in hospital three months.

She wrote to her dad in Australia and told him a lot of lies. He said she was a liar. And she told me he was cruel to her with the strap. I hated him and his wife. Anyway I had a letter where he said he would send the money for her to come back. She went to live with a neighbour. I never saw her again. As far as I know she went to live in Australia again. I tried to get in touch and went through the British Embassy, but we had lost their last address and without it they can't do anything.

My second husband went to hospital first with sciatica and had to be on weights. When I was in my last job I was gradually losing weight. I just thought it was because I was working. It turned out I had a thyroid gland. My eyes were like two frogs popping out. It was my turn to be ill and I was really poorly. I had hallucinations. I thought I was on a plane all on my own and thought all the doctors and nurses were angels. Before I went into hospital I was making tea all the time. My mind was racing like a fast clock speeding round. I was in Ramsgate hospital for seven weeks. Once when I went for a walk in the grounds I went into a hedge full of thorns and sat down. I thought a robin was God and the cat was the devil. I was still hallucinating. I used to crawl on the floor in the ward thinking I saw cockroaches and I used to be laughing one minute and crying the next. It all felt so real. I thought when I went into hospital that I was going mad and I would never come out. I went to have treatment in the psychiatric hospital for four weeks. Then I came out. I was still having treatment for my thyroid until we moved to York.

Mum and my step-dad retired from the guest house and we went to live in a house in Westgate, which was not far from Westbrook. I hated the house. It was old and I felt it was haunted. We did the house up and had a new kitchen, knocked down the wall between the two rooms, had a new suite and TV, carpets, cabinet, bedroom furniture. We were only there not quite a year and my step-father took ill. He was so poorly and lost weight and had a lot of pain. I used to go downstairs as he slept on the settee. I got ill myself and went to hospital, had treatment and I was a bit aggressive so they put me in a padded cell for a few hours with my nighty and just a mattress. One of the patients slapped my face, but she was ill herself.

I did not know at the time my step-father was dying of liver cancer. He said if he gets over his illness we would go and live in the North near my brother. I came to see my step-father. He was very thin and looked ill. I came out of hospital and a fortnight after this he died. Mum and I were so upset as he was unconscious and never woke up. He was only poorly for about five months, it was so quick. He had just got his pension and just turned 65. We did the rest of the house up and sold the house in Margate and went on a cruise after selling. A house I had lost – two homes and two marriages plus my children. I was never happy in Margate.

Chapter Seven – Came to Live in York

It was 1990 when mum and I came to live in York. The first year in October mum found a lump in her mouth. It was cancer. She was petrified. She had to go through such a lot. She had treatment, radiotherapy, for about 21 days. She swore and could not eat because her mouth was full of ulcers. I used to go into the other room and let her get it out of her system. But before that we had some nice trips with Eddy Brown coaches and went to Scarborough on holiday. She went a while and she had a lot of operations.

After three years I met a wonderful man and we became very good friends. We went on trips in the car. We went on holiday to Scarborough and I was ill and he took me back to York. I was stamping my feet and singing and crying. We were having such a good time. We went on the ghost train and on trips on a speed boat. We were having such a wonderful time when we came back to York. I had to go to the doctor and he sent me to hospital. I had tablets and was in for about three months. I hated it, seeing all the other people poorly when I was getting better. I wanted to get out.

Mum had one op after another and she had cancer in her arm. She had such pain I wanted to take the pain from her. She used to be sick and it broke my heart that she could not eat.

Towards the end she had a split in her pipe so she could not drink; she had to have mashed-up foods. If she had drunk, it would have gone in her lungs and could have killed her. In between times we went on holidays to Jersey and Scarborough.

My brother was a teacher and a great artist, played in a band and rode motorbikes, plus flew kites and gliders. He was very clever and bright. He helped us a lot in the house, put up a kitchen plus other jobs. Mum always loved the garden but could not do much. She could not use her right arm so I did everything. I had to blend all her food so she could eat it, even a little crumb she could not eat.

My brother got ill; he had prostate cancer that went to his bones. He did the gardens front and back. He lost weight like mum who was only 5½ stone. He was ill for three years and went into hospital and had treatment. He had four blood transfusions. There was no cure for him. I used to go with my boyfriend to visit him and his daughter visited him nearly every night. He was in hospital for six weeks then went into a nursing home. Sometimes they had no morphine or food so the daughter had to go and get it from the shops.

Mum went into hospital as well. She could not walk and had also broken her hip a few years ago. Her legs swelled up. My brother went into a hospice and then a nursing home. He was so weak and poorly and sick all the time until he had a syringe driver. He fell and had a black eye. It was heartbreaking as you could not do anything. I did his washing also mum's. He died on the 23rd June 2001 and my mum died two weeks after on the 6th July. My brother was buried and mum was cremated. I was devastated. I called out and cried for weeks. Mum used to say don't fret for me as you can't bring me back. My boyfriend and my niece were great and helped me through my grieving. He is so understanding and lovable – do anything for me.

After the funeral I had another crisis. The house was not in my name so I had a year of worry. I was poorly again and in hospital. My niece who is a doctor says that I get manic depression so now and then I get ill and I take medication and I am on anti-depressants. I see a nurse every week or every fortnight now and a doctor once every three months. Now I get out and go with my friend to the pop-in and with my neighbour, who is very good to me and kind, to bingo. I will go to Sycamore House in a month's time. I was very high and then depressed in hospital and withdrawn when I came out. I was still very withdrawn and depressed for about two months then I had the tablets and slowly got better. I dressed mum and bathed her for 11½ years I looked after her.

This is a true story; no names are mentioned to keep it private. This is written in my own writing. So now I am well and happy and contented, so I have to watch that I don't get ill again if I can help it. I don't know how my life will end. I have also been suicidal three times in my life but there is always a light at the end of the tunnel so never give up on yourself or life as life is worth living. This book is mainly for people who are like me and have a nervous illness and to prove that if I can do it, and I have, so can you and others.

The end.

Manic Depression

Manic: Very happy could do anything. Get up in the night, switch on and off the lights, talk loud, clapping hands, pull the curtains open and shut, want to go out through the night, keep looking out the windows thinking I am somebody else, thought I was God, shouting, singing aloud, got lost and did not know where I was. Brain went so fast I was trying to do everything at once. Wiping things over again and again, waking up people in bed in hospital, pacing up and down thinking I am matron, open cars really believing I was in control with the world not being able to concentrate. After the manic...

Depression: Very sad, unhappy, crying, withdrawn, wish I was somebody else, things don't penetrate, suicidal, don't want to live, don't want to talk, want to be on my own, throw things, fling myself about, self-inflicted, hitting out at people, aggressive, lost confidence, had panic attacks, don't want to eat, can't sleep.

CLARISSA
or
ARRESTED INNOCENCE

By

Jennifer Sinclair Robertson

Chipmunka Anthology Volume Six

Published by
Chipmunkapublishing
PO Box 6872
Brentwood
Essex CM13 1ZT
United Kingdom

http://www.chipmunkapublishing.com

Edited by Mary Dow

Permissions

The following poems have appeared in *Uninvited Guest, a family's journey through schizophrenia*, Jenny Robertson, Triangle/SPCK 1997 who have kindly given permission to use them here:

Like dew, dancing; House facing winter (also published in Loss and Language, Chapman Publications, 1994); *Overdrive; O, the Owl…* (also Chapman Publications);
This mystery…(Options); Drawing class; Breakdown and remedy; Care plans; The wound in your mind; Bone of her bone (Am I?) Snowdrops; Be; Vain charm; Non-existent life; Therapy group; Bus ride; Avalanche (Destruction); Reverie (also Chapman Publications)

Chipmunka Anthology Volume Six

Contents

32. The way to write
33. The waste of war
34. Good Friday, St Petersburg
35. Warsaw courtyard
36. Reverie
37. Clarissa's summer song

Clarissa, or arrested innocence

Snowdrop slender, Clarissa grew;
loved small, defenceless things.
On wave-washed shores traced angels' wings
where the hermit-heron flew.

Her hair shone in the westering sun.
No one feared the night to come.

She watched a timid otter dart
among seaweed covered rocks;
saw seals play in mackerel tracks;
painted seascapes - innocent art!

Soared sunwards. Too close to searing flame
her mind was scorched, perceptions maimed.

Showers threw down sunlit spears
on pasture, hill. An April lamb
brought breech to birth! Clarissa came
trembling home with joy, in tears.

Ill-wished, a blighted rose, she fell
at sixteen beneath an unkind spell,

thoughts trapped in jangling carapace
whose whorls wire messages which race
down tangled paths where wild beasts pace.

"That policeman has a tiger's face!
Stop taunting me! Get off my case!"

Now nothing can undo this curse;
no gallant prince, no tender nurse,
just drugs and needles - yes: by force!

Overwhelming tides toss Clarissa out and in:
bewildered selkie in a cruel skin.

A cruel skin

'There's that evil police car again!
The Law keeps damaging my brain...'
She seldom
reveals thoughts jangled in her disturbed mind
and so I press
this proffered shell against my ear,
although I scarcely hear
the whisper of a wave, far less
the sounding of that overwhelming sea
whose surges bore her far away from me,
tossed her, bewildered, out and in,
a damaged selkie in a cruel skin.

It is a discordant carapace
whose whorls are wires which hum and buzz
She listens, smiles.
Her eyes betray the things she cannot tell.
Pain paints angry contours on her face:
'Go away! Get off my case!'

I match my footsteps to her spaced-out pace.
Storms stole her lovely pearl,
cast back a plundered shell.

Like dew, dancing

We wished no ill-omen
at the dawn of her being,
in the garden of her babyhood
where dew dances in sunlight.

There are always thorns in the rose garden.
Briar Rose, in a place cleared of cutting edges fell
under the curse

at bud-blossom sixteen.

But no one breathed a word,
of the shadow to darken *her* rosebud life
unfolding before us

like dew, dancing

Silhouette

The evening sun slants through glass
to touch your hair.
Your mind is full of the sound of the sea.
You have glimpsed the shy otter
at the end of the rocks, have heard
seals sing, seen heron and curlew fly.

Soon you will stand against the horizon,
ringed with fire,
an in-gathering of islands.

House facing winter

Choosing the sunshine, I try to forget
she's in the shadows, sleeping at noon-time.

I try to find comfort in bird-song, waken each morning
to cadences carolled from branches and bushes
while she is shuttered in her summer of stupor,
a full-blown June rose, beautiful, blighted,
living with me in this house facing winter.

The sun doesn't brighten our windows, visit our garden.

Overdrive

Her biker brother's racing handbooks state,
'Don't rust survival instincts to negate
the risk of hurt. Helmet and leather gear,
well-planned tactics protect far more than fear.
To keep top speed, extend and dip the knee –
you graze the ground, but note: the human bone
is weak, may break beneath a mere three stone,
so ride and learn your limit is the key.'

Yet when the brain goes into overdrive
no tricks of track can help the self survive,
no cambered roadway keeps rash thoughts on
course,
just drugs and needles – if need be, by force.

The psyche's pitch is finely tuned, refined:
no physic's found to mend a broken mind.

O, the Owl is a baker's daughter…

The mind, mind has mountains…
the self – caves.
You felt your pit-props slip;
and we only knew we'd lost you
into a twilit existence,
entombed in a bedroom grave.

Life has pricked you sore,
your mind's fingers bleed.

Once you ran
over sunlit shores, sang
to seals, swam,
turned cartwheels across the sand.

It was Eden then.
Your fair hair shone in the westering sun.
We knew nothing of the night to come,
did not fear the snake.

The roses of your womanhood
are eaten with this blight; the garden
you once tended is overgrown with weeds

The music you danced to, the songs,
the friends you used to call
all turned off, in this long
unfriendly silence.
No rosemary for remembrance,
no heart's ease – only rue.
The owl is a baker's daughter.

Can young girl's wits be mortal?

I cast for comfort I can no more get,
never now see your blond head
among the crowds in Princes Street

among the crowds in Princes Street
are folk in wheelchairs; guys who sit
with placards, begging a meal, a bed,

but your boots no longer stride, your head
tosses on your pillows, haar or sun or wet
I cast for comfort… can no more get.

You wept.
We listened to a litany of loss
day and night, night and day.
'No one can feel
what's happened to me. This is for real…'

When you were small
I carried you over cliffs,
laid you in a hollow,
that the earth might be your cradle,
April sun hold you.
You lay content,
eyes like quiet stars.

Talitha, koum…
I give you this rune:
Let lark song restore you,
warmth enfold you,
love blossom again.

Icarus

'My country - chaos,' her pen-friend wrote
from Russia. 'Crimea, once Paradise,
a sun-steeped playground, rich in vine and fruit,
a microcosm now of our demise,
provides no outlet, nothing to inspire.
I'm trapped. A moth in amber petrifies.
My mind's too frail to fight corruption's mire.'

Clarissa's hurt is seen in haunted eyes.
She too is trapped, and voices, demons jeer.
For if, 'We thought our life a sparrow's flight
from dark to dark, we knew not whence nor where,
save this brief sojourn in feast and firelight...'
she, brilliant, soared too close to searing flame,
then fell in ash and shadow, grounded, maimed.

Drawing class

'I can't draw a cat,' Clarissa said,
wiping out her third attempt,
'until I know its anatomy.'

Tutored thus, I understood
I had not studied the bones
on which I fleshed my trust.

Amateurs assume too much.

A botched-up job does for the real thing.

The artist stands back
          - and starts again.

Breakdown and Remedy

Once, conversation was a good ordering of
possibilities.
The commonplace pulsed with melodious sounds.
Now, words are stones -
no hospice for my wounds.

Comfort is too spare,
but crumbs are not denied the poor.
The store of the destitute – of necessity – is bare.

Yet where there is no voice, no one is dumb;
where there is no choice, less may equal some.

Care plans

Officers – on paper – are in place
but fail to pass
the haunted wilderness
where a young woman chain-smokes,
locked in inner space.
Unopened mail floods her untrodden floor.

I am pinioned on a hackneyed metaphor.

'Who will deliver me?'

'Psychosis,' says an expert,
'is not a benign state of mind.'

Clarissa writes, 'Who will deliver me from darkness,
respect me for my rights to be?
O, to be in the Highlands where red deer run!
How I love to play on the sands
where little ones go with their mummies and
daddies to be free
summer-long by silver seas,
far from criminals and prisons, ransacking and
injustice.
I love to see the snow fall softly
across streets and houses and towns
where there is no noise but the sound
of muffled cars. The mind
has many mountains. Sometimes
it is respected, sometimes known,
but often I feel it is being completely destroyed.'

Experts state, 'It's so complex.
There's no predictive test.
We need to go slowly and carefully. There's the risk
that funding will fail or stigma block
the path of progress.'

The tabloids write, '*Miracle cure*
brings thousands hope. Help for the mentally ill.'

Her doctor says, 'There is no doubt indeed
that your daughter is very ill, but she is rather poor
at remembering to take medication. We must bring
her back
into hospital, but in all honesty
I do not think she will ever return
to her previous level of function.'

Clarissa cries, 'What's left for me?
I want to have my own self back.
I 'm not going to survive.
I look at the world.
I see no compassion, just a hard brick wall.'

The authorities write, 'Difficulties in providing
appropriate care are, of course, cause for concern.
Our Trust acknowledges that your daughter is not
well maintained,
but every effort is being made.
We are committed to patient care, we recognise
patients' rights to treatment designed around
individual needs.
However, these improvements take time...

Clarissa pleads, 'Mum, when will I get out of here?
Three whole years! It's absolutely ridiculous!
You don't understand the pain I'm in. I'm depressed to the point of death.
I have interviews, phone calls. No one comes up with anything.
I want to have my baby. I want to have a home.
Please help me, Mum. It's horrible in here.
The medication makes me ill but they don't care.
They drug you to the eyeballs but they won't let you sleep.
They barge into the bedroom and yell, 'get up!'
I've been through so much I can barely manage to be.
Mum, do something about it. Mum, help me.'

Her doctor writes, 'I always find it difficult
when a relative of someone I see professionally
tries to be more helpful than the person themselves would wish.
But thank you for your interest in the widest possible sense.'

Clarissa concludes:'I'm going to get free of this Section.
I try to speak to the doctor but he won't move on it.
Nobody listens to me. They treat me like a nothing,
a piece of psychiatric shit.'
The wound in your mind refuses love

Rowanberries tinge the bright years of your lost girlhood.

You tell me beauty has a bitter taste.

A secret smile flickers across your face.
Your words are sharp with hurt.

The wound in your mind refuses love.

There is no key. You are locked in, fast.
The sea is a wild dream, madness of foam.

If he hadn't looked at you, his eyes holding yours as he spoke words of love. It was the look that took your heart, the gentle words, praising your goodness.

You ordered your wedding dress, white as winter seas, held lace
finer than spin-drift against your throat. The cloth is half-sewn.

Tangled thoughts twist fraying threads. The fabric crushes, comes undone.

My swan princess, your lost self is lovelier than any dress.
Yours are the pools and islands of the west.
Fly again

Bone of her bone…

Summer rain streaks
the barred window-pane.
Mascara runnels her cheeks.

‘Am I *mad*?’ she whispers.

I am close as her heart’s breath
Yet I cannot reach her,
adrift on the deeps.

Together we affirm
etched on a scan,
the shape of her child, forming within –
bone of her bone, fibre and brain.

Outside, the wind weeps.

Frailty is strength which makes us kind

You felt your baby burgeon and begin
her hidden life, unfurl, a tender leaf,
an embryonic print across a screen.
Her perfection assured you that her life
is worth the swollen months, the throes which join
our human race; for those who lack, and those
who have enough must rear their young, must learn
uncertain grace notes: love and hope. The rose
which blossoms from the bud shows what we are,
though prickles tear, mildew and maggots blight.
Our risks, our hurts, mistakes, still chart the star
we aim for, graph our path through dark and light.

Your little daughter teaches, foetal, blind
that frailty is strength which makes us kind.

Snowdrops

She grew slender as a snowdrop,
loved defenceless things:
seals, and that tremulous pearl
the ebb of summer light leaves
where waves have been.

She traced angels' wings
on stone and cloud

at length blossomed forth
her own dear sundered bud.

Each spring in city gardens
snowdrops defy the winds of winter,
light lean Lenten flames.

These storm-tossed flowers
are not more brave and gentle
than a young mother
required to relinquish
the child of her heart.

Clarissa's call

Your nursery still catches the morning sun,
although your cot has long since gone.
New-born baby cards, one by one
dropped from the empty wall –
and all because I made that call.

They say I'm not well, but it's not true;
wherever you are, you know it too.
I called because I care so much for you.
A mother always knows what's best to do!

That phone call voiced my concern.
The police were planning to storm our home,
tamper with your precious brain.
I had to keep you safe from harm.

The authorities took action without delay!
"An ambulance is on its way.
Put Baby in her little sling.
It's time for long-term fostering."

I'll never forget that disastrous day.
Your eyes, when they drove you away
looked so helplessly back at me –
I sensed you knew what was to be.

I tried to guard you from a world gone mad,
protect you from everything that's bad:
powerful voices, banging-shut of doors;
footsteps tramping down long corridors,
care orders, control by force.

I gave you safety with my mothering,
and now your birthday has come round again;
but today, as they thrust that needle in,
something happened, such a sweet, secret thing
 -    like brush of angel wing:
                                        I heard you calling
and felt my own heart sing.

Enduring Loss

November light drains from a leaden sky
against an interlace of naked boughs.
Leaves gusted in gales when winds were high:
Now neon lights play cat's cradle with bare trees.

The birthday of Clarissa's child draws
to its close. Our year's end has no party gloss.
Separated by scaffolding of court procedures, laws,
we are mute and motionless, enduring loss.

Trapped within tangled wires of discordant dreams
no flight path transports us to kindlier climes.
We share a photograph fading with time:
the natal bed where, on this day,
a newborn baby and her blissful mother lay.

Be

Be content
with space and silence,
a lesser flight

for a girl, grounded.
Be glad
of conversation, the grace
of being. Together –
and no word said.

Yes, and the late light of midsummer
washes the peaceful harbour,
balm for troubled soul.

Rejoice: she is your daughter.

But, oh, if she were whole…

We would remember
loss no longer,
unlock lark song, laughter,

stretch forth untrammelled hands,

B E

Vain charm

My name means sea-water,
foaming, white.
I would wash you, my daughter,
whose name means bright,
would purge from you forever
delusions and fear,
be your white witch to charm
your hurt, your harm,
weave words of delight about your hair,
undo all the darkness,
release you, young are you are,
restore you your motherhood, your own baby dear.

But words have no potency,
well-springs no flow,
love has no meaning
in the non-life where you go -
only hard needles, a mask
to dampen despair. Therefore I ask
forlornly for healing – heavens are brass,
good words mere mockery
and your sweet youth has passed
into the shadows
while others go free
you are stranded
with no recovery.

Sorrow

'Where shall I put sorrow?'
pondered God,
searching though infinity
for star or stone.

'Let it be hard, let it be sharp or dull,
but let it take sorrow's form.'

The stars sobbed, 'No!'
and the weight of sorrow crushed the stone.

Then God put sorrow in a tree
whose branches trembled against wild skies.
'This is too heavy,' moaned the tree.
'Wood will crack and bend.'

God gave a woman a song for her womb
and the woman bore this load.
Her man bent his back to carry God's sorrow home.

'It is our birthright,' he said.
The woman replied, 'It is my children's bread.

'So, tree shelter us, wood warm us,
stone guard us, star guide us
as we take sorrow for our own.'

Locked out, locked in

Spacious dwellings once built for the well-to-do
become hostels for those who can no longer do,
whose bodies function, but brains are broken.

Clarissa homes with four dulled males.
Her eyes are closed, booted feet rest on a chair
- she'll always break the rules.

'Shall we see your room?
My voice is false and bright,
just such a tone cajoles a child into nursery,
coaxes the aged into care.
Three years old or ninety-three
resist, powerless to flee.

'It's locked,' Clarissa says.

Locked out, locked in,
reduced, mind-wounded, overcome,
evicted, homeless twice;
held down, forcibly injected
an army of key workers, support workers,
community workers, social workers, consultants,
lawyers...
'Why?'

No reply.

Schizophrenia's not the tragedy it used to be...
Community care, better attitudes, drop-in groups,
better medication...

Clarissa says with anguished eyes, ‘It’s a lie.’

Total tartan

Clarissa leaves the hospital through an open gate.

She passes a guy in a kilt, Black Watch tartan.

She sees so many poor souls drift in and out of here,
ramshackle men and lumpy women, but never one in total tartan:
the pride of Scotland gang agley.

His long hose slide in wrinkles down skinny, milk-white legs,
green flashes flap behind.
A tourie with crazy ginger hair tops him oddly off.
His left hand, splayed and twisted jerks at his side.
He talks non-stop, an aggressive drone.

Clarissa too walks with medicated gait.
Her maroon fleece has been picked from some one's laundry basket. She pulls the hood down like a cowl. Her tattered jacket reveals ill-assorted clothing underneath.

Must mental illness mean relentless decrepitude?

Inside the clock

'I'll put you on hold,' the receptionist says.

I am always on hold now,
Let down, stood up – it doesn't matter…
I'll wait – and pay the parking fees,
phone bills; extensions are endlessly belled.

The key-worker's busy; the doctor's not on the ward today; the social worker's on holiday; we've had a lot of staff changes, but we're doing our best to put a package of care together…

Put on hold as years drip away,
waiting for the wonder cure.

Nothing moves forward, except the clock,
Clarissa's source of fear.

'I'm scared…'
'Scared? Why?'
'It's that nurse. She's always here, telling me what to do.'
'Where's the nurse, dear?'
She withers me with a look.

'She's inside the clock, going tick, tick, tick.'

Non-existent life

'Why do they give me medication?
I have a God-given right to total health.'

There are no rights in madness,
though the law allows appeal and claim.
Illness over-rides dictates of reason.
She is gravid with never-ending phantoms,
swellings last not months, but years;
her energies are directed to delusion of birth-giving
- non-existent life.

Therapy group

A meeting place for minds
much buffetted;
a place of calm, no pressure,
space to explore, to make.

Making mends frayed ends.

When communication fails
we fondle cats –
or reach for a pen.

Here there's humour, coffee, encounters, friends.

Busy people keep appointments,
draft agendas, plans,
make profits, ulcers, doubtful gains.

There is solace in this meeting place of minds.

Baroque flute in a museum

Its wood is warm as amber.
It lies here dumb
beside black notes on yellowed paper.
The hands which coaxed sounds
through honeyed rounds are bone.
The lips, persuasive instruments, are mute,
nor seethes the genial mind,
transforming melody from marked notation.

Centuries drift dust and guidebooks.

Will some traveller
pass custodians' muster,
defy all thorny regulations,
kiss the empty mouthpiece,
waken the silent flute?

Bus ride in counterpoint

A passenger on a mid-morning bus
I muse on relationship and loss,
recall a melody, haunting as a flute:
'*And thou away, the very birds are mute…*'

The bus stutters forward with a jolt.

I glimpse the latest news:
'Bevvied Hazza gets the boot from curry house.'
The metre splutters a belly-laugh, slapstick,
alliterates, troch – a -ic.

The bus pulls to a halt.

Such contrast of mood and sound
means a poem will be found
to weave its pattern through the daily round

now

alight.

Destruction

First, an avalanche:

Clarissa's engulfed.

Then, an explosion
left her derelict
in rubble where windows gape
and walls collapse.

Clarissa asks 'why?'

She thought she had no pen –
and so she missed a poem.

She crossed the road too quickly
- and caught the wrong bus.

She chose the wrong menu
in a coffee shop.

She asks, 'why?'

and because there is no answer
we mourn that poem
which might have been
- but never was.

To set words free

It's simple to pin words down:
pick up pencil or ballpoint pen -
an inexpensive tool.
Your fingers bend at will.
You learnt the way at school.
easy as ABC.

But to set words free
to take shape, make permanent,
or effervesce and float,
and randomly delight -
this is the way to write.
The craft is carved with scalpels, cut
from some unknown, burning stone
with a cost all of its own.
This work has no price or wage -
but words sing on the page.

The waste of war
(Schizophrenia has devastated more lives than all the wars of the last centuries.)

An lost army, half a million boys and men, froze,
their bodies pierced to the deep-chilled marrow
on retreat from Moscow through relentless snow.

Britain rejoiced with pealing bells, crescendoes
of choirs exulting, 'The Lord be praised!'
Russian genius caught the epic in mighty prose
and overture, but Poland grieved, erased.

The ground was too hard to dig the army's grave.
Their bodies were thrown into defences they had hewn
earlier that year on their long route from the west.
Country children, hair white as blossom, had cheered
them then. Old women had blessed
each mother's son. Bison had stirred in ancient lairs.
On wide wings storks returned to waiting nests.

Last year bulldozers unearthed the bones
and debris of those defeated men,
whose teeth, starved, had sucked on stones.
Recruits and drummer boys still in their teens
were analysed, then laid to rest among tall pines.
Oaks scattered wreaths of autumn gold.
Birches shook out an amber requiem
for regiments whose flags had unfurled
like blossom in May, whose marching men

saw neither spring, nor summer come again.

Good Friday, St Petersburg

Amidst crowds of passers-by
a man falls and cannot rise,
a woman holds out a plaintive hand,
a girl and infant huddle on the ground:
the child's eyes accuse
the careless multitude.

Too easy to compare this with that day when wood
held fast the riven flesh of an unresisting man,
his agony exposed to public view.
But we may suppose
the beggars here no different from those
who drifted, beseeching alms, about the crowded hill;
nor other were the drunks who tossed the dice;
nor is the grief of women any less
who mourn a father, husband, brother lost
in mindless conflict in the east;
a daughter in madness, a child in pain
now… or then.
A busker makes mournful music in the underpass
and crowds –   press on.

Warsaw courtyard: the moorings of memory

Women sit contentedly in the kindly sun.
This is their final home,
a many-windowed building of honeyed stone
an erstwhile convent, cut off from town.
That busy world is no longer even a distant hum.

The place is graced by a name: Caritas.
The women are the recipients, saggy bundles
in motley hand-me-downs.
No one has much now to call her own.
The charity is in the peace
of gnarled hands at rest on faded dress.
There is anchorage and quiet haven here, giving
space
for small things: sulks and pettiness;
and smiles and well-worn reminiscence.

One woman sits apart.
Her sleek brown head does not belong,
it seems, to the general throng.
She clutches warm, black beads.
The moorings of her memory have gone
and the rhythms of the rosary, like a childhood song
comfort her as she drifts, placidly, along.

Sometimes foreigners encroach upon her enclosed
space,
strange beings from some fabled place;
and then she is most anxious to please.
'Anglais? Francais?" she enquires, and serenades
her visitors with 'La Marseilleise'.
And now we see a book-lined salon,
glasses of golden tea, and a young girl brought in
to charm her mother's guests
with songs she learnt from her French governess.

The melodies still sing, though words are lost.

Reverie

(a poem for Clarissa, after a painting, *Giovanina seated on the window sill*, Pawel Tchiastiakov, 1864, Russian Museum, St Petersburg)

Her eyes tranquil with reveries,
a girl muses, becalmed. The sky's oyster shell
beyond rooftops reveals its luminous pearl.
Her window is open to the first glimmer of dawn.
She is morning's sentinel: vigilant on the sill
she views, not distant vistas, nor shadows below,
nor mists, drifting, dissolving – her gaze is within,
guarding thoughts all her own. She does not know
her reflection shimmers, mirror-like in the pane
against which her shoulders repose. Seated so,
she is glimpsed by a painter, early astir,
who spreads out his canvas to capture her dream.

Clarissa's summer song

Enfolded by islands,
clouds, seals, sea
are Coll and Tiree.

Deep-moulded horizon,
hills hung with mist,
one shore sun-kissed.

Dreaming lone islands:
wide skies welcome
high hills of Rhum.

Mull and blue Uist
with scattered Treshnish
strung in the midst.

Islands of the west
by greed dispossessed,
Tir-nan-Og ever blessed.

Islandscape of dreams,
adrift on the sea,
Eilean mo chridhe.

MASHED MIND

Poems

By Suzanne Eley

Chipmunka Anthology Volume Six

Published by
Chipmunkapublishing
PO Box 6872
Brentwood
Essex CM13 1ZT
United Kingdom

http://www.chipmunkapublishing.com

Edited by Danielle Atkins

Introduction

I have Bipolar disorder with rapid cycling; at times it is great as I seem to be able to achieve so much. But the real problem for me is the deep depression. I have suffered bipolar as long as can remember; the first signs for me raised its ugly head when I was about 7 or 8.

I began to feel alone and different and had no idea what was going on. I could not understand why I felt so depressed yet nothing in my life had caused me to feel so bad. No one then even really knew about bipolar so that was not even considered. Because of this lack of knowledge I certainly have suffered more than I should have done.
I did not get my diagnosis until three and half years ago, I was on lithium for a while but could not handle feeling normal as it was such a long time ago that I knew what it felt like. For me it is still a constant struggle and I have tried to live as normal as possible.

I would like to see more understanding of mental health issues and to see more help out there, the waiting time is dangerously long, a lot can happen during that wait. I would also like to see the entire stigma dropped; there are amazingly still some doctors that seem to have little understanding. Thankfully mine is great.

I have written many poems over the last few years whilst suffering many mood swings of my bipolar.

I have suffered with this over many years and this has caused many life changing things to occur in my life.

Some good and some scary times have come from it.

I spent three years in a boarding school as a result.

I have some how managed a fairly normal life and now have children.

I am tempted to write about it one day, maybe I will you never know.

I have started a forum for use of any people who may which to speak to others with such like times.

Find me and the forum at

http://bipolarndepression.myfastforum.org/

I dedicate this too my very much missed Dad,

And too my log term partner Rob for sticking with me
through all my moods.

DREAMS

Dreams are like a butterfly,
Who live life up so high.
Among the clouds and the trees,
Living life with no disease.

Dreams are sure to mystify,
The people that just cannot fly,
But please my friends do not cry.
For dreams will come when you fly.

WONDER

I lay awake at night,
Dreaming in a haze.
Thinking of what's in sight.
Into the darkness I gaze,
Hoping to see the light,
Why is life a maze?

LOVE

A warm feeling in the heart,
Living life in a dream.
You don't want it to depart,
That loving feeling in your heart.

MAKING HAPPY

When things get hard,
And you can't cope.
Relax your mind,
And smoke some dope.

Turn on your stereo.
Put up the base.
Then put that little thing called,
Called a smile in your face.

Pictures in your mind,
Tell you of a better place.
The future that's ahead,
And the past?
That's dead……

WAR

Words of war we hear,
Help! We live in fear.
For the life we love,
War turns it to mud.

For on we are all trampled,
All we want is peace,
That's too hard to ask.
As our dreams are crumpled.
Our life that goes so fast.

THIS WORLD

We are killing our world,
Suffocating our trees,
Starving our pets,
Spreading disease.
For when will we learn it must end?
For this world, on us depends.

WHY

The days go by,
Life carry's on,
You ache inside,
Wondering why?

You know the reasons,
It doesn't make sense.
Life seems so cruel,
You feel so tense.

The clouds go by,
You watch the sky.
Wondering, waiting.
Knowing we all must die.

TIME

Tomorrow is another day,
Yesterday has gone.
Live life for today.
We cannot change a wrong.
Forget all bad,
Remember the good.
Enjoy your lives
You know you should.

UNWANTED

Here it comes again,
That unwanted pain.
It hits you hard,
Like a speeding train.
I drew the wrong card.
When will it go again?
This unwanted pain.

WALKING ABOUT OUTSIDE

Hearing a giggle,
Are they laughing at me?
Hearing them talk,
Are they talking about me?
Seeing them stare,
Wishing I weren't there.
That paranoia follows you everywhere.

GONE AWAY

The pain I feel,
Is deep inside.
The dream I see,
Has gone away.
The pills I take,
Will end this day.
Everything will go away.

Lay down my head.
World becomes a haze.
Darkness falls,
I wait for death,
I drift away,
Never to see another day……

A VICTIM OF THE FREEMASONS

By Walter Taylor

Chipmunka Anthology Volume Six

Published by
Chipmunkapublishing
PO Box 6872
Brentwood
Essex CM13 1ZT
United Kingdom

http://www.chipmunkapublishing.com

Edited by Kimberley Bishop

This is a unique story, an unprecedented story, an absolutely true story.

I intend to make it a short, brief synopsis, having written a book, "The Price of Truth and Justice", which was published in April 2003. I have also written a manuscript of a story entitled, "The Freemasons Unveiled'' which, as yet, I cannot get published.

Now it doesn't take a rocket scientist to fathom out the reason I can't get it published because the freemasons are everywhere, in all walks of life as I will explain later, consequently this resulting in me writing this short synopsis, which I hope to get published quickly and cheaply so that it will sell well at a low price. Any profits will go to charity. Cancer Research etc. as I have enough brass until I pop my clogs.

Speaking from experience the freemasons are a very large, powerful, unelected, undemocratic, corrupt secret underworld involved in malpractice and wrong doings. I am referring to North Wales Police, solicitors, clerks of the courts, magistrates, barristers, Q.C.'s, judges, town councillors, an ex high sheriff and also my three doctors, G.P.'s over the last fifty five years. (They stick together like s..t to a blanket.) Incidentally, I have dissociated myself from my current G.P., a freemason, for fear of a Doctor Harold Shipman. I could name them all, with pleasure, but publishers are terrified of libel, yet there is nothing libellous in my true story, which I could voice in the highest court in the land. Consequently, I well delete their names in this short synopsis for the time being.

The object of this short synopsis is to prove how I, after twenty one dedicated years in my profession and becoming a first class craftsman carpenter and joiner which included:

- Two years national service
- Military conduct, very good, insufficient service to qualify for exemplary
- First Class craftsman carpenter
- A good N.C.O. - full corporal <u>who could get work out of others</u>

Also nine years with one of the biggest civil engineering contractors in Great Britain and gaining promotion to the position of general foreman sub agent placed on the staff and superannuated.

I resign from this great firm for the specific reason of our two sons' education, as they had been in six different schools (not a bad judge as one is now a Senior Lecturer in Law and the other a Director in Graphic Design). I then get a job as charge hand joiner employed by N.C.C (Nuclear Civil Contractors), everything going perfect, offered promotion to foreman joiner.

I then became a victim of a clique of bad, evil scum of the earth liars and was dismissed for <u>alleged bad timekeeping and unsatisfactory work.</u> This was nothing but lies, <u>false, defamation of character.</u>
<u>IT WAS LUDICROUS.</u>

I had documents, statements and witnesses to prove everything. I then became a victim of bad, evil, irresponsible, negligent union officials. I then became a victim of a young, inexperienced, incompetent solicitor. After giving it careful consideration and being at a financial loss I took the law into my own hands to bring this evil lot to court to have them exposed. I ASSAULT TWO OF THEM. I then became a victim of bent, evil corrupt police officers, court officials, magistrates and this young, evil, Judas solicitor who betrayed me.

I was then made out to be a criminal monster from blatant lies on oath and placed in custody in Shrewsbury prison aided and abetted by the police and this Judas of a solicitor in league with them. Most of these police, solicitors and court officials (unknown to me) were staunch freemasons, as I will explain later in my synopsis.

As an 82 years young senior citizen, I, Walter Taylor, retired and live in our recently built, three bedroom, detached bungalow, situated in this beautiful market town of Bala, Gwynedd, North Wales. Living in my twilight years with plenty of time on my hands in between golfing three days a week, gardening, a little cycling and walking and taking my dear wife Eunice on holidays three to four times a year.

It is imperative to emphasize that I knew nothing about the freemasons until the late nineteen nineties and 'by gum' have I gathered some interesting material to reference the corrupt malpractice and wrong doings carried out by this powerful, undemocratic, unelected secret underworld, the freemasons.

The object of my short, brief synopsis, although a David and Goliath job will be crystal clear, something constructive, i.e. not only to expose this secret organised body but also to bring to an end, to abolish the freemasons, because in this modern age of 2006 there is no place in any democratic society for any secret organisations full stop. It was a different kettle of fish 100 to 150 years ago when the working man wasn't so educated as today. Anyway, any human being who is prepared to stoop and join a secret organisation is not to be trusted. Decent masons resign as soon as they learn that it is a scam, i.e. secret meetings, secret signs, helping upper classes to get preferential treatment etc. For the benefit of the general public like myself who knew nothing or very little about this secret organisation they were at one time approximately 700,000 strong:-

Approximately 40,000 in Ireland
Approximately 60,000 in Scotland
Approximately 600,000 in England and Wales, including members of parliament and royalty.

I have good reasons, evidence and experience to mention that North Wales, especially Bala was more densely populated with freemasons than anywhere else in the United Kingdom. That is taking into account of per head of population of adult males. I am also informed by a reliable source that there are over one hundred lodges in the North Wales area.

Incidentally I am just one of very many of a great number of citizens from various parts of the United Kingdom (too many to mention) from London, Kent, Bristol, Birmingham, Liverpool, Cardiff, Camarthen, Aberystwyth, Pwllheli and Glasgow who have been victims of the freemasons. They are all organising meetings (anti Masonic) in different parts of the United Kingdom, which I support 100%, as a matter of fact I have sent cash to support three of these organized outlets.

However, very, very briefly, I will now explain the genuine, proper, relevant, legitimate reason for me writing this short synopsis, which gives me great pleasure.

2004/5

As an 80 years young senior citizen living comfortably and keeping fit, in a recently built, three bedroom, detached bungalow, which is paid for, no mortgage. In good health, thanks to the Great Man Above, the Governor, The Architect of the Universe. Having reduced my playing of golf from four times a week to a couple of times a week, with a Mr. Terry Evans, a golfing fanatic, and a Mr. Alan Phillips, a senior citizen, 80 years young and still enjoying his golf.

1924

I was born at No. 2 Ney Street, Waterloo, Ashton-under-Lyne, Lancashire, 12th August 1924. My Mam and Dad were a very hard working, devoted couple. My father, who had served in the 1914-18 war was also a coal miner. Whilst working underground at Woodpark Colliery, Bardsley, Oldham, Lancashire, he had one of his legs crushed and this turned septic. He then caught pneumonia and died, this leaving my dear mother with five children to bring up herself with very little money coming in. Needless to say I had a very hard, tough but honest childhood. I was informed that Dad was a sporting type, taking part in football, boxing and running. He also kept chickens to supply new laid eggs for the family.

1928

Attending Christ Church School, Waterloo, Ashton-under-Lyne, having only a scant education yet still passing exams to go to high school – but my mother could not afford it.

1928/1938

Having to go to work in a cotton mill, the Belgrave Spinning Mill, in Oldham, Lancashire. Started as a ‘reacher over’, very quickly promoted to ‘oiler’. Forced to leave as I caught a skin disease from the oil. I ended up in Ashton-under-Lyne infirmary very ill, very low. I nearly kicked the bucket.

I make a quick, miracle recovery, discharged from hospital, spent a few days convalescing.

1938/40

Began to serve my apprenticeship as a carpenter and joiner with one of the best, finest, highly skilled joiners around. His name was Mr. Clem Walworth of No. 30 Beautrice Avenue, Reddich, Manchester. A great foreman joiner. He was an artisan at his profession. He arranged for me to attend Heginsbottom Technical College, Ashton-under-Lyne, Lancashire three nights a week. Passed my exams in: -

- Woodworking Practical)
- Woodworking Theoretical) Diploma enclosed
- Geometry and Calculation)

PATRON: HIS MAJESTY THE KING

UNION OF LANCASHIRE AND CHESHIRE INSTITUTES 1943

WOODWORKERS' COURSE

FIRST YEAR

THIS IS TO CERTIFY THAT

Walter Taylor

PASSED THE EXAMINATIONS OF THE UNION IN THE FOLLOWING SUBJECTS

Woodworking (Theoretical)	First Class
Woodworking (Practical)	Second Class
Geometry and Calculations	Second Class

(18/9 7th Nov 43)

Leverhulme

PRESIDENT OF UNION

Bertram B. Slater. — CHAIRMAN OF COUNCIL

[illegible] — SECRETARY

1943

Attending same college, studying for second year. My mates join the forces, go to war. I volunteer for the Royal Navy, Royal Air Force and the Army. Am told that I am deferred because of serving my apprenticeship as a carpenter and joiner. As I can't get into the forces and want to do my bit for my country (against the wishes of my foreman joiner and Mr. Preston, personnel manager) I volunteer to go working down in London on bomb damage repair work. It's a very dangerous job.

1943/44

I have two narrow escapes, one with a V1 doodlebug and one with a V2 rocket. Also, attend London Polytechnic, Holloway Road, London for City and Guilds Intermediate.

1944/45

We celebrate V.E. night in London pubs and Buckingham Palace. War ended return back north to my birthplace, Waterloo.

1946

Called up for National Service, two great years – cross country running, physical training, small arms drill including bren gun, sten gun and rifle, represented the army at football, table tennis and cricket.

1948

I was then 'demobbed,' Army record reads "Corporal Taylor, Walter – Military Conduct Very Good, insufficient service to qualify for Exemplary. A 1st. class carpenter and joiner, a good N.C.O. who worked hard and cheerfully, who could get work out of others." I have army release book as proof.

RELEASE LEAVE CERTIFICATE

Army Form X 202/A

Army No. 14153773 Present Rank CPL.

Surname (Block Letters) TAYLOR

Christian Name/s WALTER

Unit, Regt. or Corps A. A. Command School of Tech. Instrn., R.E.M.E.

Date of : ~~Demobilisation~~

*Calling up for military service 11 April 46

* Strike out whichever is inapplicable.

Release leave expires on – 6 JUL 1948

(a) Trade on enlistment App Joiner ~~(Carpentry)~~ (Joinery Building)

(c) Service Trade Carpenter & Joiner

(b) Trade courses and trade tests passed Carpenter/Jnr I

(d) Any other qualification for civilian employment —

Military Conduct: "VERY GOOD" (insufficient service to qualify for "EXEMPLARY")

Testimonial: A very good carpenter who worked hard and cheerfully. A good NCO who could get work out of others

Unit overseas or U.K. Stamp: A.A. Command School of Technical Instruction R.E.M.E. 11 MAY 1948

Place Crookham Date 11 May 48

Officer's Signature [signature] Major

Signature of Soldier W. Taylor

UK RELEASE

* Army Education Record (including particulars under (a), (b), (c) and (d) below). This section will not be filled in until receipt of further War Office Instructions.

(a) Type of course (b) Length (c) Total hours of Instruction. (d) Record of achievement.

(i)*

(ii)*

(iii)*

(iv)*

* Instructors will insert the letter "I" here to indicate that in their case the record refers to courses in which they have acted as Instructors.

Signature of Unit Education Officer..........

POSITION OF SOLDIER ON TERMINATION OF RELEASE LEAVE

1. A regular soldier with Reserve service to complete will be transferred to the Royal Army Reserve, and will receive Reserve pay until his period of Reserve service has been completed. If on that date the Emergency still exists, he will cease to draw Reserve pay, and will then be transferred to Army Reserve Class "Z" (unpaid).
2. A regular soldier who has completed his Colour and Reserve service engagement will be transferred to Army Reserve Class "Z" (unpaid).
3. All other soldiers will be transferred to Army Reserve Class "Z" or Class "Z" (T).

SPECIAL NOTE.—Army Reservists are liable to recall to the colours, if necessary, during the continuing period of the Emergency.

Notes:

(i) Further details of service and of medals to which entitled may be had on application to O i/c Records, accompanied by the applicant's A.B.64, Part I.

(ii) If this certificate is lost or mislaid, no duplicate can be obtained.

(iii) Any alterations of the particulars given in this certificate may render the holder liable to Prosecution under the Seamen's and Soldiers' False Characters Act, 1906.

THE ABOVE-NAMED MAN PROCEEDED ON RELEASE LEAVE ON THE DATE SHOWN IN THE MILITARY DISPERSAL UNIT STAMP OPPOSITE.

N.B.—A certificate showing the date of transfer to the appropriate Army Reserve (A.F. X 202/B) will be issued by the Officer i/c Record Office.

Military Dispersal Unit Stamp. No. 11 C.M.D.A.D.C. 11 MAY 1948 ALDERSHOT.

A very proud day.

Photograph taken in the city of Bath 1947, shortly after I was promoted to full Corporal 1st Class Carpenter at 23 years of age.

(This, obviously, before I became a victim of the secret Masonic organization)

Eunice and I on our wedding day, 22nd July 1950

1948

Arrive in this beautiful town of Bala, building houses in Bro Eryl. I meet and marry one of the sweetest, smartest, prettiest attractive eighteen year olds that God ever let live. She was also very hard working, loads of common sense and very honest.

1948

A very special day, 22nd July 1950 – we marry.

1950

We buy a small, dilapidated terrace cottage, No. 6 Castle St. Bala through our solicitors, Donald T.R. Jones, for £165. We work hard and make it into a little dream home. My dear wife gives birth to our two special sons. I mention that bit about my wife – very honest – because of a bad, evil, corrupt coward of a B-----d police inspector, William Hughes Parry, who made my dear, devoted wife believe that I, the father of her two little boys, her devoted husband, could be up for murder. He put her in a state of shock. I will explain in detail at the appropriate part of my story. This happened on the night of 26th October 1960. To me it happened yesterday. He was nothing but a henchman for a tyrant of the North Wales courts, Harry Evans Jones, a solicitor, a police prosecutor. This happened when they dumped me in a police cell. Both staunch chapel people, both staunch freemasons, both corrupt cowards. They were a disgrace to our world renowned British Justice system, a disgrace to our world renowned British Police Force. As a matter of fact, I have written a manuscript, "The Freemasons Unveiled – The Silent Destroyers," as yet I can't get it published. All this is therapeutic, however, back to my synopsis.

1951 to 1960

Employed for 9 years with one of the biggest and best civil engineering contractors in Great Britain, John Laings & Sons. Started with them as a joiner, they promoted me to charge hand joiner, foreman joiner, general foreman. I was placed on the staff and superannuated, promoted to sub agent, a job for life. I resign from this great firm for the specific reason of our children's education, as they had been in six different schools. I receive a great reply letter from L. Laings, how sorry he is to loose my services. I hold and cherish these documents as proof.

Feb 1960

I get a job as charge hand joiner, employed by N.C.C. Nuclear Civil Constructions on the nuclear power station site, Trawsfynydd, working seven days a week, 8 a.m. to 7 p.m., 65 hours per week (accumulating one of the best gangs on site, these were the words of the A.S.W. Union steward), making very high bonus payments. Was asked to take promotion to foreman joiner (again I have witnesses and wage slips as proof).

End of |August to October 1960

Now here is where my wonderful life, my 31 years of 'God made nothing nicer,' 21years of dedicated, keen and conscious work, successful years in my profession and becoming a first class joiner, with documents and witnesses to prove it without an atom of doubt, and meeting and marrying a gorgeous girl in a million. My whole life changes completely. I become a victim of three deadly dangerous, irresponsible liars, Smith, Neads and Fox. It is a long story but I remember it as though it was yesterday. At approximately ten minutes to 3 p.m. on a Friday, August 1960 Bill Neads came to me on the Number One Reactor site and said, "Wally, I've got some bad news for you." I said, "What is it Bill?" He said, "You will be finishing tonight." I said, "That's O.K. but you must give me a reason." He then said, "I think its bad timekeeping and unsatisfactory work or something." I said, "What on earth are you talking about, me a bad time keeper and unsatisfactory worker or something! Do you feel alright?" He then said, "Look Wally, you know you are not a bad timekeeper and unsatisfactory worker and I know you are not a bad timekeeper and unsatisfactory worker but it's not me who is sacking you, it's them." I said, "Why don't you be a man and speak the truth?" At that he walked away. As he walked away I said, "This is not the last you will hear of this you know!"

I then put my case through every channel in my power. The management of Nuclear Civil Constructors (N.C.C), the union A.S.W. (Amalgamated Society of Woodworkers). The senior A.S.W. Site Steward, Dick Dugdale agreed with me 100% as it was nothing but a pack of lies, it was wrong, it was false, it was defamation of character, it was ludicrous. He said, "If they will sack you Wally, they will sack anybody on site and we will go the distance with this one. I said, "Thank you Dick." Now, very briefly as I could write a dozen pages of how I put my full case to an A.S.W. Area Delegate, Albert Prest, who turned out to be a double agent, in league with the management. I was re-employed (under protest) by the same company, N.C.C., as a joiner (not a supervisor of joiners) on a different section of the project.

I approach a young, 20 odd year old solicitor, Huw Lloyd Williams in Mount Street, Bala. I ask, "Do you deal with industrial matters?" He replies, "Yes, what is it?" Now, over a period of seven to eight weeks I describe to him in a full, comprehensive detailed manner, from A to Z with documents, statements, a diploma and names of witnesses plus my wage slips proving my good timekeeping and high bonus payments and excellent work over a period of 21 years, plus the actions, and negligence of these double agents, union A.S.W. officials.

Mid October 1960
26th October 1960

Now, this young, inexperienced Judas of a solicitor ends up telling me he's been in contact with this union delegate, A. Prest. Again, very briefly as I could write a few pages of how I described this double agent union delegate, A. Prest and these scum of the earth liars, Smith, Neads and Fox, I end up saying to this solicitor, H. L. Williams, "What do I have to do to get these liars and union officials exposed and dealt with?" The solicitor looks at me and shakes his shoulders. I say, "If I was big enough and strong enough I would like to go on site and give them a damn good hiding and bring them to court that way!" The solicitor says, "I wouldn't advise you to do that." I say, "No, I've got more oil in my can (more sense)." He then gives me back all my important evidential documents. I remember it as though it was yesterday, walking down the stairs in his office with all these documents in my hands never been used.

After putting my case of wrongful dismissal through every channel in my power (as I have explained) and becoming a victim of evil cowards, liars of N.C.C.(Nuclear Civil Constructors), a victim of A.S.W. (Amalgamates Society of Woodworkers) officials, a victim of a young, inexperienced, incompetent solicitor and being at a financial loss of about £32.10 shillings (which was quite an amount in the old money in those days, the 1960's)
After giving it very careful thought I decided to do something to get this scum of the earth lot into a court to get them exposed and dealt

with, to prove I was not a bad timekeeper and unsatisfactory worker, to prove I was a good timekeeper and a very good worker.
Now this is exactly what I did on the evening of 26th October 1960. I saw this bloke Smith, the creator of all this case, the cheater, the coward, and the liar. He was about 25 to 30 yards away. I was de-nailing a piece of 2 x 2 timber with my joiners nail extractor. He appeared to be looking over a concrete wall spying on someone. I ran over to Smith and said, "You dirty, rotten liar. How can you stoop so low and sack me for bad timekeeping and unsatisfactory work you liar!" I then attempted to hit him on his shoulder with my nail extractor, just enough to hurt him, to cause an affray so that I could get him to court and have him exposed as a liar and a cheat. I must stress, *and this is very, very important,* I ONLY HIT HIM ONCE. Unfortunately, the blow missed his shoulder and caught him on the side of his head. I am not sorry for what I did and will never apologise for it. (See sketch plan below.)

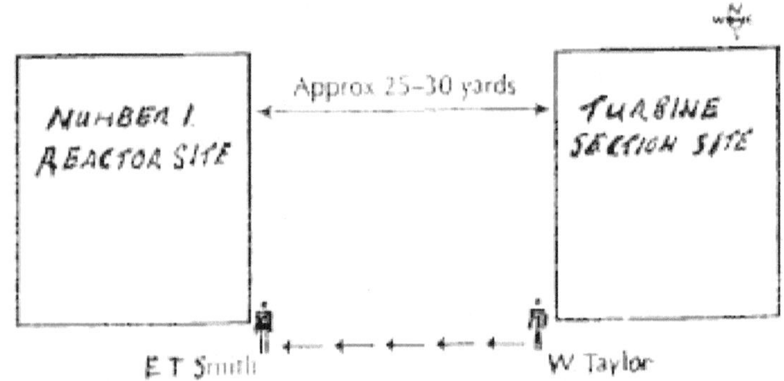

26th October 1960

I then said, "Where are your partners in crime, Neads and Fox?" Then I went looking for Neads and Fox. I saw William Neads on the access scaffolding on the south end of the No. 1 Reactor site and walked towards him (see following sketch).
I said "Eh, Neads, come here." He said, "What do you want?" I dropped my nail extractor and jumped up the steps and said, "Have you got no truth or principles in you?" He said, "What do you mean?" I said, "You know what I mean, carrying those lies from Smith to me and sacking me for bad timekeeping and unsatisfactory

work! You liar! When you had told me yourself I'm not a bad timekeeper or unsatisfactory worker." He again said, "What do you mean?" I then hit him with my right fist, as hard as I could, in the region of his mouth. It was a beauty. He fell like a log to the floor, to the scaffolding boards. He then got up and stuck a finger in my right eye. I then got hold of him around the waist and squeezed him as hard as I could and said, "I will squeeze some truth into you, you liar!" At this time I felt as if I had the strength of a tank.) He then shouted, "Aw!" and pulled my hair. I then said, "You are not worth hitting again! Where's you partner in crime – Fox? I will give him a punch while I'm here." He said, "He's on holiday." I said, "That will save me from giving him a punch." I then walked back off the scaffolding to the ground (see sketch plan below).

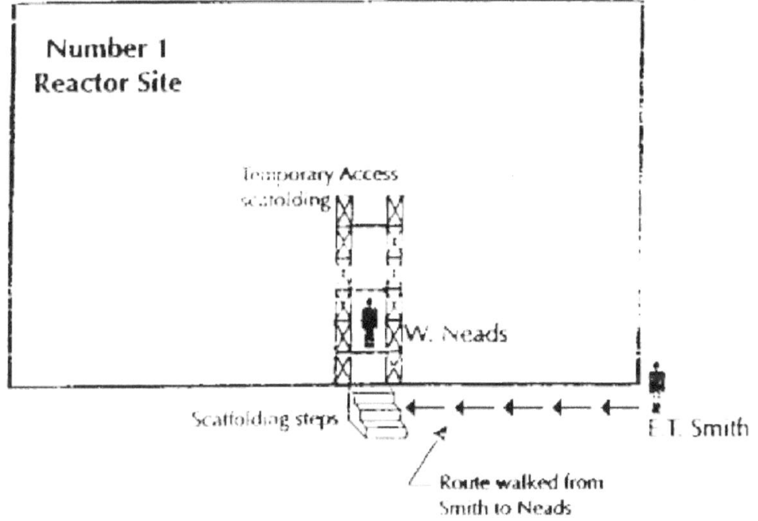

26th October 1960
At this point Ian Birrell appeared. He was part of this clique of Smith, Neads and Fox. Ian Birrell said, "I will challenge you to a fight!" I said, "You are a couple of stone heavier than me but I have

a brother at home who is just about your weight and he's a professional boxer, he will take you on and knock some truth into you. We have a professional referee in Trawsfynydd and the proceeds can go to Cancer Research." At that Ian Birrell shut up. At this stage I had a good feeling, a wonderful feeling of satisfaction. I had taken the law into my own hands and I was looking forward to my case coming to court and having these men exposed as liars. I also thought that the betrayal of the union officials who had failed to clear my good name and the inexperience of my solicitor would be shown up and dealt with. I had faith in the British justice system. I knew that I had done wrong, obviously expecting my reasons for my actions to be put to the court. Police constable Watkins arrives on site; I put my full case to him on site. We travel from site to Blaenau Ffestiniog police station, no handcuffs, we are chatting together like two mates. He asks, "Will you make out a statement?" I say, "Yes, certainly." He then writes down my long, detailed, truthful, honest, comprehensive statement covering my case and my life from A to Z, from the day I was born (12th August 1924) to the present late evening, 26th October 1960. I am still very confident, never been in a police station or court procedure in my life. P.C. Watkins then asks for my car keys, gold watch, £6-10 shilling in the old money and then says, "You will get these back." He then puts me in a police cell, takes away my bootlaces. I then ring the cell bell and ask, "Can I speak to the police officer in charge please?" Along comes Police Inspector Parry. Again, very briefly, I then explain to him my full case from A to Z. He asks, "Have you got a solicitor?" I say our solicitor is Mr. Donald Jones, as my wife, Eunice, and I bought our stone cottage, No. 6 Castle Street, through him in 1950 but I have put my case to a solicitor, H.L. Williams of Bala who has failed miserably as an industrial matter. Police Inspector Parry, "Do you want to speak to him?" "Well, as he knows all about my case as an industrial matter, I can do." Police Inspector Parry goes to the phone and says, "Mr. Williams is on the phone if you want to speak to him." I say, "Hello Mr. Williams." Mr. Williams says, "You've done it now." I say, "Done what now?" Williams doesn't answer me. I say, "Are you coming to see me?" Williams says, "I can't." "Well, can you get a message to my dear wife Eunice and tell her to come to the police station at Blaenau Ffestiniog and not to worry as everything will be all right." I am now put back in the police cell. Police Inspector Parry comes to me and says, "Your wife is here to see you." Walking behind Parry from the cell to my wife Police Inspector Parry says, "Do you know this man's skull is only the thickness of an eggshell. You could have killed him." I say, "Do you know this man Smith has got a thick skull. He should have thought about that before he wrongfully sacked me for bad timekeeping and unsatisfactory work and robbing me of £32.10 shillings financially." Police Inspector Parry did not answer me, he walked through this door and I followed. My dear, devoted wife Eunice normally looked very smart, very attractive, with a lovely smiling face. In complete contrast she was in a state of shock. She looked gaunt, haggard, she was shaking nervously. She collapsed on me crying and saying, "Wally, what on earth have you been doing?" I caress her, hold her and say, "Why love?" She says, "I've just asked that police officer, 'How are the men?' and he says it is touch and go for one of them." I say, "Don't believe him love, he's telling you lies, he's making this case worse than what it is. He is Police Inspector Parry." Eunice goes home crying, in a taxi with a strange driver, 22 miles over the mountains to Bala, I go back to the police cell. Shortly after Police Inspector Parry came to the cell and said, "Come with me!" I follow him to the courtroom and this is what happened, late evening on the 26th October 1960.

On the 26th October 1960. (See sketch plan below) This is what happened in the courtroom that night.

An old female bitch in league with corrupt police, solicitors, Freemasons

Clerk of the Court

A Tyrant
A Freemason
A Coward

William Hughes Parry

A Freemason
A Coward
A Liar

Completely on my own, no defence solicitor

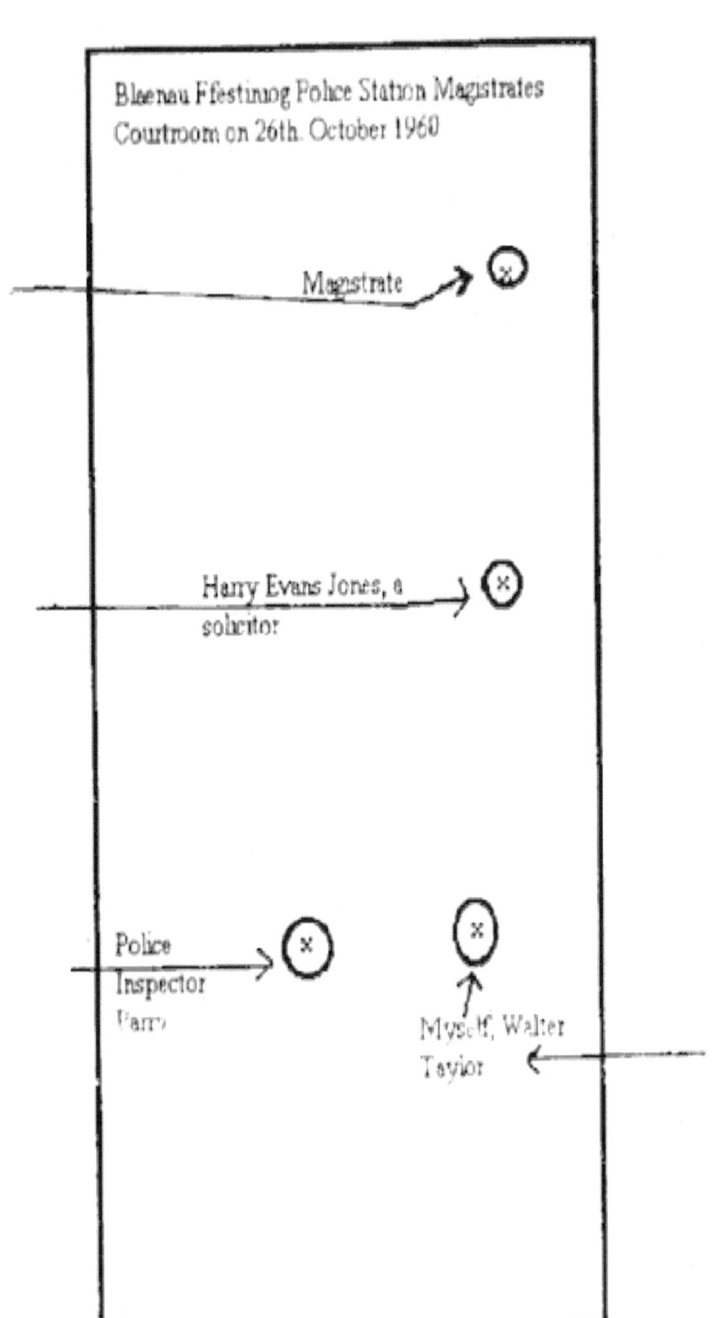
Blaenau Ffestiniog Police Station Magistrates
Courtroom on 26th. October 1960
Magistrate
Harry Evans Jones, a
solicitor
Police
Inspector
Myself, Walter
Taylor

H. E. Jones, in a loud, stentorian, frightening voice shouted, "You will be charged with 'Grievous Bodily Harm with Intent to Ernest Thompson Smith' and 'Occasioning Actual Bodily Harm to William Neads,'" then, in a threatening, challenging manner he shouted, "Have you got anything to say?"

I said that I would like my long statement read out. Police Inspector Parry retorted, "It's a long statement. Anyway I haven't time." As he said this he waved the papers, my statement, in his right hand. I said, "It's a long statement, a very important statement. It matters a lot in this case, I would like it read out. Then H. E. Jones shouted, "Shut up and don't be cheeky." The elderly female magistrate, who had witnessed everything, immediately said, "You will be remanded in custody." I then broke down and cried and said, "It's four years since my mother died." I then walked back to the police station cell.

I'm finger printed by Sergeant Ben Evans then handcuffed to a young police constable and another young P. C. driving, taken twenty odd miles to Bala then handcuffed to another P. C. and on the train to Shrewsbury Prison.
During this 14 days this tyrant police solicitor, H. E. Jones and this bent, corrupt coward police inspector, W. H. Parry and this Judas of a young, twenty odd year old, so called defence solicitor (in league with the police), H. L. Williams, were organizing and planning the Magistrates Court Committal Proceedings, with the help of police prosecuting solicitors, magistrates and nine prosecuting witnesses, (including two doctors, one crane driver, one engineer and a pump man). None of these had witnessed anything at all. All this organizing was carried out whilst I was stitching mailbags in Shrewsbury Prison, where they had put me in custody. During this fourteen days my dear wife had taken all my very important documents, evidence including a diploma, my exemplary military record, my experience of being General Foreman Sub Agent, my good timekeeping documents and witnesses statements of me being

placed on the staff and superannuated, to this Judas of a solicitor sat on his arse in his grubby little office, 60 Mount Street, Bala.
I am escorted from Shrewsbury Prison in a taxi with two prison wardens and the taxi driver and taken seventy odd miles, still in my working clothes, donkey jacket and boots. I arrive at Blaenau Ffestiniog magistrate's committal proceedings. I change into my best suit, shirt, tie and shoes (a very smart lad in those days). P.C. Watkins comes into the cell and puts my tie straight (a nice man so far), he says, "Your solicitor is in that room." I go into the room. The solicitor, H. L. Williams, says, "How much money have you got?" I say, "I'm not telling you how much money I've got. You should be asking me more important questions. You should be asking me what has happened between Smith and I and Neads and I. How can you defend me if you don't know what has happened?" This Judas, H. L. Williams, solicitor, then went to the anti room, obviously to speak to the tyrant solicitor clerk to the court, H. E. Jones. Again very briefly in court 9th November 1960, against me there were two police officers, nine prosecution witnesses, two police prosecuting council, a police tyrant court clerk plus this Judas solicitor H. L. Williams who was supposed to be defending me. He was in league with the police. That, in Basic English, is fifteen versus one (see sketch plan on next page).

I had never been in a court in my life!

I was made out to be a criminal monster, degraded and dumped in Shrewsbury Prison, not one of my two dozen or so defence witnesses were in court. My dear wife and my family and myself could never understand it all.

I knew nothing about the Freemasons at the time. I did not know they existed. They destroyed my life! This is a classic case of Masonic ill treatment. I wrote a book, 'The Price of Truth and Justice,' launched April 2003. It cost me £7,800. I've written the manuscript of my second book, 'The Freemasons Unveiled,' (which I can't get published as yet). "Pretty Obvious!"
These are extracts from my second book. This is only the tip of the iceberg. Still to come - the Masonic controlled

Dolgellau Assize Court (16th January 1961) plus more Freemason controlled courts.

Blaenau Ffestiniog Magistrates Court

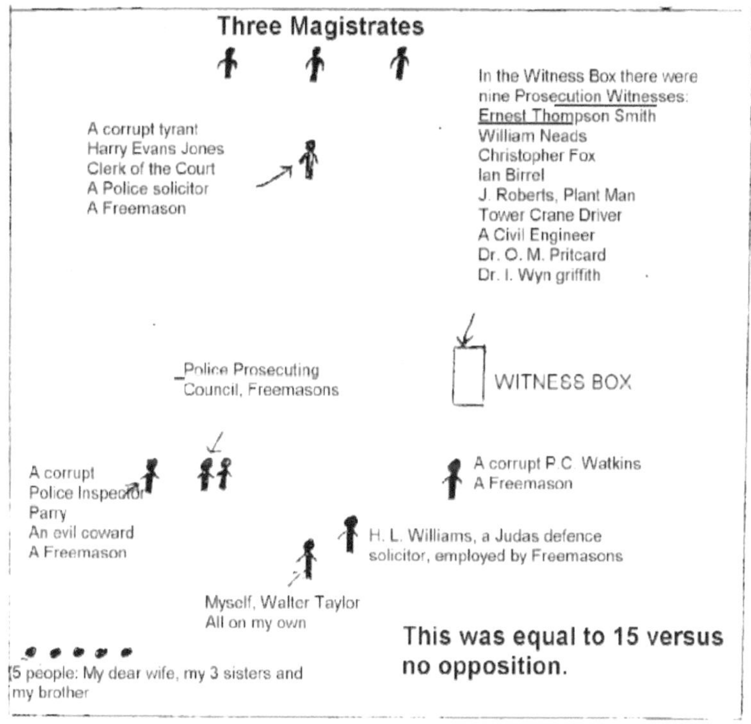

Monday morning 16 Jan 1961

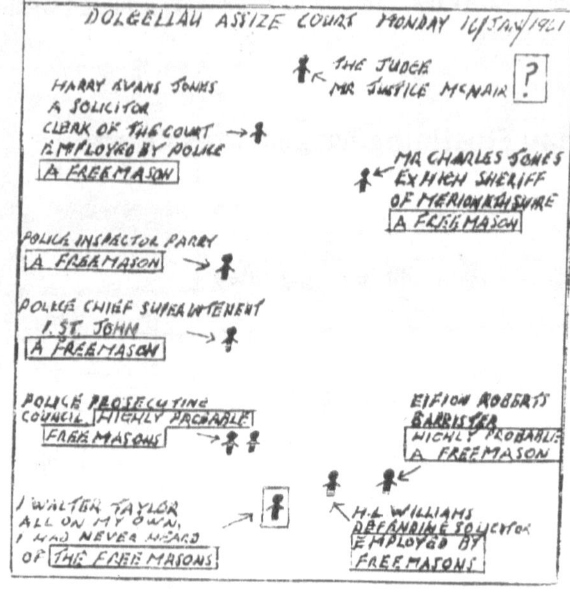

Just before the assize court started, before I stood in the dock, Dick Dugdale, the senior Union Steward came to me and Said" I'm sorry Wally, I've come to confess." His confession was kept from the freemasons.

16A

COPY OF LETTER FROM KEY WITNESS TO DEFENDING SOLICITOR WHICH NIETHER WERE USED IN COURT

R. DUGDALE,
7, THORNTON CRES,
MORECOMBE
LANCS..
/1960

MR. HUW LLOYD WILLIAMS
SOLICITOR.

Dear Mr Williams,

I was more than surprised when I read your letter and learned of the trouble concerning Mr W. Taylor at Trawsfynydd. However, I do remember very well the case of Mr Taylor being dismissed for "BAD TIMEKEEPING" and "unsatisfactory work.

When he put his case to me it was obvious that certain people at the site were anxious to get rid of Mr Taylor because he had made such good progress as a chargehand foreman with an excellent gang, this had put other chargehands and

foremen in a bad light, therefore Mr Taylor had to go and in my opinion was provoked into taking the action which has led to his present position
It is ridiculous to even suggest that mr Taylor was anything but and efficient and concientious charge-hand, who had earned high bonus payments, with his gang and had previously worked for John Laing in the capacity of foreman Joiner for many years, before having to return home to facilitate his childrens education.
On Civil Engineering Sites, jealousies and 'cliques' are rife and I would definitely say that Mr Taylor was

3.

the victim of this pitfall. In view of the fact that I know "What goes on" and having met and followed the progress of Mr Taylor as an H.S.W. member and a I was the shop steward for the H.S.W on that site at the time, I am quite prepared to come to court and quote the above on oath and perhaps other pertinent facts regarding Mr Taylor's unfortunate dismissal

Yours Faithfully

R Dugdale.

8 pm.
Friday 13th
Jan 1961

Monday
morning
16th Jan 1961
I have to demand an appointment with a barrister. I don't see Eifion Roberts, barrister, until 8 p.m. on Friday night, the 13th January 1961 before my case at the assize court on the following Monday, 16th January 1961.

Just before the assize court started, before I stood in the dock, Dick Dugdale, the senior Union Steward came to me and said, "I'm sorry Wally, I've come to confess." His confession was kept from court by Freemasons.

THE ASSIZE COURT PROCEEDINGS

H. L. Wil liams hurried to me and said, in a very serious, strained, quiet, voice, "Just say 'Not Guilty' to occasioning bodily harm, and just say 'Guilty' to grievous bodily harm." I said to H. L. Wil liams, "No. I'm **Not Guilty** to the lies which were told on oath by prosecution witnesses, at the magistrates' court in Blaenau Ffestiniog."
Eifion Roberts, the barrister, then said, in a strong, powerful manner, "**THIS IS SECTION 20 Of OUR BRITISH LAW. JUST SAY 'GUILTY'.**"
At that my stomach turned, I felt sick and faint, I was in shock, forced to plead 'Guilty" to lies told on oath against me. I was forced to tell lies against myself. **This barrister, Eifion Roberts, later became a British judge.** Can you imagine this animal, this barrister, in charge of British courts, deciding the lives of human beings? This, to me, happened yesterday. However, being in shock, I don't recall what I said, but 1 must have mumbled something.

16th January 1961
The next person to speak, to my complete surprise, 1 did not know he was coming to court, was Mr. Charles Jones, an ex-High Sheriff of Meirioneth, the Mayor of Bala town council, a chief officer of

the crown, **another mason.** He said, "I know Mr. Taylor, he is a well-known man in Bala, he is not a loner, he is known to go in the pubs and have a pint with the boys. He is well respected, a devoted 'family man' and he is an above average worker."
The next thing – the very next moment this solicitor H L. Williams, turned round to me and said, "Don't say much." I was left flabbergasted - overcome with shock. I just stood there in the dock unable to speak. I had been looking forward for weeks to telling the judge everything. The circumstances were so contrary to everything that I had expected from British justice.

The next person to speak was the barrister, Mr. Eifion Roberts. In a very clear, accurate manner he said, "Mr. Taylor is thirty six years of age, he is a married man with a wife and two young sons. He is a devoted husband and father, he is no ruffian, he has not got a blemish on his character. His friends and workmates on the nuclear power station site have had a collection for him and his wife which raised £26. He is now employed as a joiner by Tarmac Civil Engineering Contractors, on the construction of the Tryweryn Dam at Capel Celyn earning £12 a week."

The judge, Mr. Justice McNair, asked, "How far is it from Bala to the power station?" Someone said, "Twenty two miles." The judge then said, "You will be discharged conditionally for two years."

I asked the solicitor and the barrister, "It's not over is it?" One of them said, "You are now a free man." I said, "What about these men telling lies on oath and the police telling lies to my wife and keeping my long statement from the court?" They just totally ignored me. I was left standing in the dock with my hands gripped tightly to the dock sides. I wanted to shout out, "This is not justice!" It took two police officers to release my tightly gripped hands from the dock sides. I was in a daze - confused and bewildered. If ever there was a case of malpractice by police, police solicitors, magistrates, a barrister and a judge, this was a classic example.

I then put my case to so many channels over the years, including local M.P's, the judge, Chief Constable of North Wales, Home Secretaries, various solicitors, grass roots. In those days, once you mentioned malpractice by police and solicitors no one wanted to know. I finished up as a voluntary patient in a mental home. "REVENGE IS A DISH BEST SERVED COLD"

I then began demonstrating, breaking windows, painting slogans on the offices and private homes and police stations. Result - they held their own private courts, secret courts, becoming their own Judge and Jury and put me in Shrewsbury Prison for eight weeks and sent a psychiatrist to me. I tell the psychiatrist to go and visit these solicitors and police; they are the ones who need a psychiatrist. I told the court I would not pay one penny of any fines, costs or charges. I was released, no charges, but look what this tyrant and his henchmen put on my conviction sheet, it's all in detail in my book. I have many sessions with Dafyd Ellis Thomas M.P. Result, he was as bent as a set of bed springs.

I carry out more demonstrations; appear in courts in North Wales on 8.12.80, 30.7.81, 3.11.81, 7.2.82, 18.3.82, and 8.5.82. More secret courts but I refuse to pay one penny of any fines, costs or damages so they send me to prison for ninety days for refusing to pay one penny of any costs. My dear paragon of a wife and mother attempts suicide, it's a miracle she was saved. We divorce while I pursue my cause. I'm 99.9% on verge of committing suicide; I could have done it as easy as walking through a door.

24th March 1965
to
25th November
1968
On 19th February 1999 I go to the private address of this Judas of a solicitor, 11, Stirling Avenue, Acton, Wrexham -I hit this H. L. Williams with my fist, in his face. Neither him nor his partners in crime, the police, took any action against me. I describe it all in detail in my book. I must come to a close, as this synopsis is getting too long.
As a learned friend of mine said, "As you are only a novice of a writer, why don't you put your story to a television or to the national

press. It could make a bomb." I said that I would welcome an interview with any of them but I wouldn't want a penny. It cost me £7,800 to publish my book. Any profits would go to cancer research.

Incidentally, I have great pleasure in mentioning that my three G.P.'s, doctors from the 1950's to 2002, were and are members of the Mickey Mouse Brigade, the Silent Destroyers, the Masons. Obviously I have disassociated myself with them, for fear of a Dr. Shipman. Now I know and understand how I ended up in a funny farm, a nervous disability centre, a mental home.

For the benefit of the millions of the United Kingdom Citizens who know nothing about the Freemasons (like myself until a few years ago), there were 600,000 in England and Wales. They are loosing thousands of members per year. Dozens of lodges are closing annually. There is no place in this modern, democratic society for secret, silent organizations.

I think it quite appropriate for the benefit of the general public that I should mention that we often read in the national press, the country is being milked of millions of pounds annually by lawyers, solicitors, barristers, Q.C.'s and judges. This, of course, is absolutely true.

But the national press, although they know, don't mention that the majority of these lawyers are freemasons.

We also very often read in the press that

THE LAW IS AN ASS

Of course we all know that the law is an ass but they don't give their reason for this, the reason being, the laws are made by members of parliament and many years ago if you were well financed or a landowner you could become an M.P if you so wished. You could be as thick as two planks or as stupid as an ass or a freemason. Consequently this resulting in – THE LAW IS AN ASS.

Incidentally, once you are a victim of the freemasons in this part of the U.K. (North Wales) you are a victim for ever, for the rest of your life.

"HO they are lovely people!"

For example:-

A couple of years ago the secretary of our local Penlan Bala Golf Club, Mr. Rhys Jones, was reported for cheating at golf on three occasions. The only punishment he received was that he was stopped from entering competitions for six months.

Now, as millions of golfers will tell you, he should have been thrown out of the club and barred for life. (Full Stop)

I complain to the club in writing (copies of letters in file) and THEY SEND ME TO COVENTRY.
I just could not understand it after being a staunch playing member for approximately thirty years
until I discover that, at the time:

- The club president, John Pritchard, is a FREEMASON.
- The club chairman. my G.P. Doctor Tecwyn Jones, is a FREEMASON (I've got rid of him
for fear of a Doctor Harold Shipman)

- The club captain Geraint Roberts is a FREEMASON
- Also a committee member Mr. D. P. Jones, a magistrate, is a FREEMASON
- And the 3 times cheater Rhys Jones is a FREEMASON

This beautiful, rural market town of Bala will be a much better place without them.

I repeat, it's all in my second book – THE FREEMASONS UNVEILED - (as yet can't get published). I'm searching for a publisher.

From an 82. year old youngster

It is imperative that I make it abundantly clear; I am not referring to our world-renowned British
Police force or our world-renowned judicial system. I am, of course, referring to the minority of
bad, evil, corrupt cowards of police, solicitors, court officials, magistrates, barristers Judges, G.P's
etc. The majority of them are Freemasons. They have cost the ratepayers thousands of pounds
illegally. They have also cost me a substantial sum of money, but, most important, they destroyed
my family. Hopefully I can get a publisher to publish this gospel truth synopsis.
REVENGE IS A DISH
BEST SERVED COLD

With Kind Regards,

W. Taylor

P.S. I have recently been very fortunate and become a (founder member of Second Family (UK)), Committed to Exposing Free-mason Corruption in Society (UK).

45 Balfour Street
Gateshead
Tyne and Wear
NE8 1YL

Hi All,

AS I promised a note of all the Founding members! I am so happy about you all and what active intelligent folk we are!

So.
Julie
Julielowe19@hotmail.com,

THE LOST HIGHWAY

By Alan James

Published by
Chipmunkapublishing
PO Box 6872
Brentwood
Essex CM13 1ZT
United Kingdom

http://www.chipmunkapublishing.com

Introduction

I recently watched a T.V. documentary about the history of country music - "The Lost Highway" I thought it was a great title for the programme as country music or as some would prefer to call it "white blues", is full of lost souls who have succumbed to depression and booze - Hank Williams and Gram Parsons to name but two who both died prematurely because of it.

However not everyone on the lost highway dies young and not everyone drinks themselves to death. This is the story of my grandparents on my father's side who regressed into Alzheimer's disease as they slowly but surely travelled down their own lost highway.

Chapter One

I was born in 1951 and my parents divorced in '55. Back in the 1950's divorce was unusual as well as traumatic. Initially I went to live with my mother and grandmother, but when my mother took ill an arrangement was made for me to go and live with my father's parents on the other side of town.

My father used to work away from home for long spells at a time as a welder on the newly constructed oil rigs, so effectively my grandparents became my parents and guardians who looked after me and brought me up.

When I went to live with them, around 1955, my grandfather was still working, as he had done all of his life since leaving school at the age of 14 to go down the pit. My grandmother had worked professionally as a dressmaker earlier in life, and though now retired she would still use the sewing machine to mend clothes as virtually nothing was ever thrown away – a harsh reminder of earlier times.

While working down the pit my grandfather caught the "miners' disease" - pneumoconiosis of the lungs, through regular inhaling of coal dust, and was transferred to the surface to work in the telephone exchange cabin, and also because of his previous experience of industrial disease he was given the prestigious job of compensation secretary to represent miners with similar industrial injuries at regional level at compensation tribunals in Newcastle.

This was a job my grandfather carried out with distinction. The miners he represented in our village all knew and respected him because of his work. This manifested itself in the late sixties when I first started drinking with him in our village. Ryhope, about 2 miles south of Sunderland, had many pubs including the "Prince of Wales" my grandfather's local, and it was virtually impossible to pay for a pint there or any other pub in the village when the locals found out you were Billy James' grandson, such was the high esteem in which he was held.

My grandfather continued to work in the telephone exchange cabin until he was 65 in 1964, shortly before the pit itself closed down. Working all his life had given my grandfather an active and productive mind. We had relations in New Zealand, and he would regularly write to them and I would read his letters before they were sent. If I had any writing skill at all I think I have inherited it from my grandfather. I went to grammar school while my grandfather at that age was going down the pit, but his letters had a long-standing effect on me as they were so beautifully written. He was a naturally gifted writer who just happened to be a miner as well.

Everything was stacked against social mobility among the working class of my grandfather's generation and my father's as well. I got into grammar school because I passed my 11 plus, so did my father but in his day he also had to be interviewed for entry into the local grammar school and when it came to the crucial interview they asked him questions on Greek mythology! In those days it wasn't what you knew it was who you knew, and that was it, my father's fate was sealed in the same way as my grandfather's.

Chapter Two

I think at this stage it is appropriate to state the obvious - I am a part-time writer not a full time doctor or medical research assistant who has found a cure for Alzheimer's, but the disease like any other has a beginning, where the first signs of the disease manifest itself and the process of mental degeneration begins. My experience with my grandparents charts the beginning of this process, and also why it happened, although I can only give my personal assessment, not a medical one.

However I think my grandfather's problems began when he retired from the work which had kept his mind active and positive. His hobby away from work was gardening, which although therapeutic was not overtly taxing. Some people enjoy and thrive on retirement but others do not, and I think my grandfather fell into the second category. Too much time on your hands which work used to occupy, and maybe this inactivity can affect the brain. It seems to me to be too much of a coincidence that my grandfather's mental deterioration coincided with the beginning of his retirement.
His daily routine changed from working 9 - 5 at the telephone exchange, followed by a pint down the local, to having a lunchtime pint instead, then going to bed in the afternoon, getting up at teatime, doing some odd jobs, and then going

back down the "Prince" for a couple of pints at night, before coming home and going back to bed. It seems ostensibly a pleasant and relaxing way to spend your time, but the brain was gradually being de-commissioned.

In the mid-sixties when my grandfather retired I was in my mid-teens and studying for my "0" levels at school. In my spare time I would be playing whatever sport was on offer, so my childhood was the same as most, except that I was the only person in my class whose parents were divorced, and in fact I had to meet someone from another school to find another person in the same situation as me. Divorce was still the exception rather than the rule back then.

While I was at school during the day and at play in the evening I hadn't really observed my domestic situation, and I suppose I was still too young then to suss it out. It didn't seem important then but domestic roles began to change at breakfast time. Like most houses in our pit village we still had a coal fire with a coal-shed at the side of the house, and my grandfather would get up early in the morning and make the fire with the remains of last nights coal, some newspaper, and some new coal before lighting it and then making my breakfast of toast, marmalade, and hot or cold squash depending on the time of year, before I went to school. However as time passed the role of provider gradually switched from my grandfather to grandmother. The significance of this escaped me at the time but now I recognize this as the first signs of malfunction on my grandfather's part. He was slowly and gradually retiring into a shell, and the self confidence was ebbing away. Although he was, in my opinion, an accomplished writer it was not something he indulged in outside of letter-writing, and apart from the "Daily Herald" and then the "Daily Mirror" (in the old days when it was a quality newspaper) he was not an avid reader, nor did he watch television. My distant memories of television in the sixties were watching "Coronation Street" in black and white with my grandmother, and also "Top of the Pops" as she was fascinated with Mick Jagger and Jimmy Hendrix!

As a typical teenager I was more absorbed in my own life rather than observing or thinking about my grandfather's decline, although if I had been more aware could I have done anything about it that would have changed things? The answer is probably not, but the reality was at that time I was blind to the problems which were beginning to surface in my grandfather's life.

Chapter Three

I passed enough "O" levels at school to stay on and do "A" levels. I had no idea whatsoever about a career, so remaining at school seemed the best option. It took two years to complete my "A" levels (from '67 - '69) and then I went straight on the dole.

At the end of '69 I bumped into an old friend from school who had just started studying at Birmingham University, and told me he had a spare room in his hall of residence as he was sleeping in his girlfriend's room, so I decided to leave home and travel down to Birmingham where I soon got a job on the buses as a conductor. This didn't last long as I was offered a job selling paintings door to door with some hippies and I moved into that bohemian environment. The office in the daytime became a crashpad at night. After a few months I suggested that some of the team could uproot and start an office in Newcastle, and after finding some great accommodation close to the beautiful Jesmond Dene, that's exactly what we did.

On the way to Newcastle we stopped off at my grandparent's house to say hello. It was mid morning and my grandmother opened the door, she told me my grandfather was still in bed, and he looked ill. I was not the only visitor as our relations from New Zealand, who he had written to so eloquently in earlier and better times, had come over to England to see him and again he was upstairs in bed, and not really well enough to receive them. While I was away in Birmingham my grandmother was observing what was happening to my grandfather and she was able to tell me about some of the things that had occurred while I was away that related to his illness.

We had always been close with both our next door neighbours, so much so that you would just give a knock on the door and walk straight into the back kitchen - in those days no one bothered to lock their back doors. On two occasions my grandfather had walked straight into Mrs Hewitt's house, once totally naked, the second time totally drenched. It had not been raining so my grandmother and neighbour could only conclude that he had walked fully clothed into the sea - which was about a mile away. He had also become incontinent and needed full time nursing, which my grandmother was totally prepared to do as a dedicated wife, but because of his rapid mental deterioration he was moved to Cherry Knowle hospital for the mentally ill, which was conveniently close by, and my grandmother would go there every day to visit him.

I used to come down from Newcastle to see him as well but he was deteriorating to the extent that he neither recognized me nor my grandmother as his relations, just someone to talk to.

My grandfather had also been a carer. When my grandmother's brother was dying of cancer in the early sixties, my grandfather used to come over to his house to shave him every week. They had both joined the army together and gone over to France towards the end of World War One, and had been great friends ever since. Now a nurse was having to shave my grandfather.

Chapter Four

My grandfather died in 1973. Throughout his illness my grandmother had been the proverbial "rock" trying her best to look after him at home, and when he became hospitalized she would walk the couple of miles to see him every day, wind, rain or shine. Apart from the obvious motives of love and devotion, caring for my grandfather had also given my grandmother something to do, to keep her mind occupied, much in the same way that working had kept his mind occupied. Now that he was dead the same mental stagnation which had blighted my grandfather in his final years would soon affect my grandmother as well.

Once again this is only my personal opinion, but the vacuum left in my grandfather's life when he retired from work was revisiting itself on my grandmother, because her work in recent years had been looking after him, and now that had disappeared with his death.

Into this equation now stepped my father. Just as my grandmother had devotedly attended my grandfather in his declining years, so my father now took it upon himself to look after his mother in much the same way. He had been working away from home during most of the sixties, when especially my grandmother was still able to take care of me, but now because she was on her own he decided to look for work closer to home so he could move back in with her. In the meantime I was still travelling around.

Initially it seemed like a good idea which both father and me were happy with as my grandmother still had her wits about her, and my dad's moving back in would stop her brooding and feeling lonely. Unfortunately, this was not to last very long and my grandmother's mental health soon began to deteriorate because I believe she had suffered the trauma of losing her husband although even in her most lucid moments she would not admit to this.

Both my grandparents developed Alzheimers but their behaviour patterns were very different. As far as I recollect my grandfather's deterioration was almost passive and introspective. When he walked into Mrs Hewitt's house totally naked he didn't say anything, and there was nothing aggressive about him to threaten our neighbour she just accepted he was ill and that was it.

However, my grandmother's deterioration was both aggressive and nasty. They say you always hurt the one you love, and consciously or sub-consciously as her illness developed she was determined to make my father's life a misery - the more he tried to help her the more she hated him for it. When I used to come to stay from time to time she would deviously try and play me off against him concocting stories of spite and hate to try to make me feel sorry for her as well as hating him at the same time. It was enough to reduce my father to tears and the whole experience was obviously very unpleasant. I kept trying to tell myself it was my grandmother's illness which was causing this and not my grandmother herself, but at times this was really hard to come to terms with, especially when I saw the effect this was having on my father's own mental health. He began working less and going down the pub more both to get drunk and try to obliterate the bad vibes, but also to spend some time away from her and keep his own sanity. She was beginning to achieve what seemed to be her aim of bringing him down to her own level.

It was obvious to me that the situation was getting right out of hand and could not continue, so I told my father in no uncertain terms that my grandmother must be hospitalized for his own wellbeing as well as hers. His self-conscious reaction was “what would the neighbours think if I put her into care” and mine was fuck what the neighbours think or you will both end up there! I spoke to Carol Wood, the social worker, about this dilemma and she eventually persuaded my father that my grandmother should go into Cherry Knowle hospital for her own good as well as his but my father took a lot of persuading as he felt (quite wrongly) that he was deserting his mother when she needed him.

As well as the verbal abuse there was the intense pressure involved with trying to look after my grandmother. It was dangerous to leave her on her own because more than once you would come into the kitchen and there would be a smell of gas, where she had turned on the cooker without lighting it.

Other experiences would be amusing in a surreal kind of way. My father would often be woken up in the middle of the night with his "Sunday lunch", as my grandmother had lost all track of time. A friend of mine slept on the settee one night only to be regularly woken up by my grandmother to ask if he wanted an egg. He would politely say no thank you, but would then be asked the same question five minutes later ad infinitum. Needless to say he only slept there once. My grandmother would go down to the post office to collect her pension, go home, and then a few minutes later would go back again. Peggy, behind the counter, an old friend, would say, "you've just had your pension Mrs James", and then she would return again a few minutes later, repeating an experience she had almost instantly forgotten or "lost."

Instant loss of memory is a symptom of Alzheimers and yet paradoxically the memory loss is of the present but not the distant past. In her most lucid moments my grandmother could recall in vivid detail memories of her distant past which were crystal clear, and would have been of great use to a social historian!

Chapter Five

When my grandmother was eventually given a bed at Cherry Knowle hospital there was a great sense of relief on my part, as it instantly removed the pressure and stress of looking after her away from my father, although I still think he felt guilty about giving up this responsibility.

It was a deja vu situation, as the same hospital had cared for my grandfather a decade previously, and my father like his mother before would undertake the daily task of visiting in all weathers to see someone who had no idea whatsoever who he was. This is the particularly cruel part of the illness - not for the patient but for the carer. When someone is physically disabled the carer is still recognized and appreciated for their attention and efforts but for an Alzheimers patient here is no response, and it is heartbreaking for the relative that they are now no more than a complete stranger to the patient. It was more so for my father than me, because he had devoted so much of his time to someone who could no longer appreciate all that he had done for her despite the vindictiveness and provocation the illness had generated along the way. Why my grandmother's reaction to her illness was so totally opposite to my grandfather's disposition is something I don't know, maybe a doctor or psychiatrist could explain why one patient is aggressive and the other passive. What they both had in common however was the same illness.

At the same time as my grandmother was transfered to a psychiatric hospital I went back to my home town to study for a humanities degree at Sunderland Poly. I finished my degree in the summer of '83 and was awarded a 2.2, which is what I thought I would get in return for the amount of work I had put in. With my father in an apparently much more stable and contented frame of mind I decided to go down to London where I found a single room in a hostel near Tower Bridge. In November there was a registered delivery for me from Sunderland which was my degree. The timing was good as I decided to go back up to Sunderland for Christmas to stay with my father and visit my grandmother. I took my degree up home for my dad to keep and proudly show to his mates down the pub. My grandmother although slightly more subdued through medication was still up to her old tricks going round the hospital rooms at night and telling the patients in no uncertain terms that they had to leave because "this was her house", which the nurses found amusing.

I left my father at Sunderland coach station at the beginning of '84, and got the bus back down to London. The next month there was a knock on my hostel room door, and it was the police. As soon as I saw them I thought "death", and it has to be my grandmother, but to my shock the police (two of them) told me it was my father who had died, definitely not my grandmother. I caught the midnight bus from London to Sunderland and went straight to my neighbour's house to find out exactly what had happened.

About twice a week my aunt Ethel, my father's cousin who also lived in the village, would call round and collect his laundry. On a given day and time my father would always be in to open the door, and after trying unsuccessfully to get in she 'phoned the police who kicked the front door in and found my father's body.

After his death my father was laid out at the Chapel of Rest next to Sunderland General hospital, so after I had been to see him I went to see the doctor who my father had visited for an appointment only 24 hours before he had died. I told him that I found it strange that someone should be allowed to leave just 24 hours before he died, but his doctor told me my father had died suddenly from a burst peptic stomach ulcer, which had poisoned his blood stream before entering his heart. This sudden trauma was called "peritonitis" and was indeed confirmed as the cause of death on his death certificate.

I took some consolation from the fact that my father had died suddenly as he had told me that he did not want to end up as a vegetable like his mother, and at least he had managed to avoid that fate. However, when my father had his final appointment he also had an x-ray on his head and his doctor told me that the x-ray indicated that the brain was actually shrinking - the first physical signs of Alzheimers. Once again this is only a personal view but I think that the pressure and stress my father had endured trying to care for my grandmother who had become a very difficult patient, had eventually taken its toll on my father as well. Peritonitis is a stress-related disease, but I think that Alzheimers may also well be in some cases.

Everyone travels down life's highway, and sometimes the road is clear from beginning to end, but when you develop Alzheimers the road becomes increasingly congested. When you go through a tunnel there is light at the beginning and end, but with Alzheimers there is only light at the beginning of the tunnel, and you gradually lose yourself in the darkness as you travel further into the interior.

My grandmother survived my father by two years and died in 1986.

Alan James
December 2006

www.ingramcontent.com/pod-product-compliance
Lightning Source LLC
LaVergne TN
LVHW091020080826
845145LV00002B/305